TABLE OF CONTENTS

14	Saavai Vendrar	67
15	Thoonguvadhu Pol	73
16	Uyirthezhundhar	81
17	Vaanamum Bhoomiyum	85
18	Vaanil Sangeetham	92
19	Vaigarai Vaaname	99

4. Other Existing/Upcoming Book By Author 103

Azhagiya Vaanil " Bb "
hahk
www.vp3.in whatsapp +91 8123235873
Transcribed By
Vp3 Music Notes & Karaoke
= 95
Bb
INTRO
PALLAVI
A zha gi ya Vaa . nil . .
A dhi sa ya Raa gam .
Aa sa yil Koo . di . .
Thoo dha ri Koo tam . A var
Paa ti ni le O ru A dhi sa yam . A dhai
Therin di run de Pudhu Ra ga si yam .
U la gil Van dha .
Me . si ya . .
1

INTERLUDE - 1
CHARANAM
me . si ya . Me . si ya . Me . si ya . .
info.vp3@gmail.com
whatsapp +91 8123235873
Ye nne Ye . nne pu dhu may Vi nnil Ke ta Sei . dhi I ni may
2 Azhagiya Vaani
2

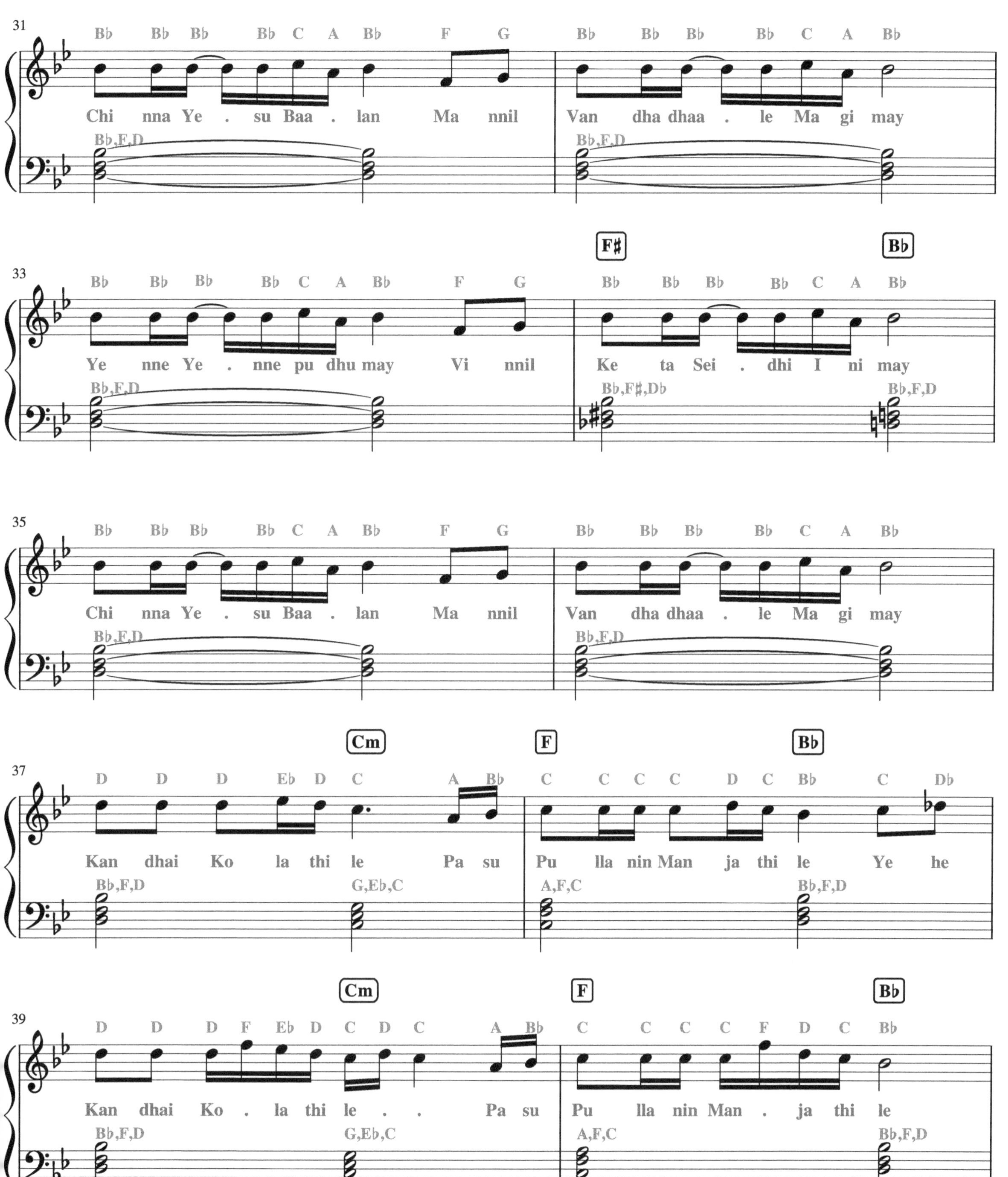

31
Bb Bb Bb Bb C A Bb F G
Bb Bb Bb Bb C A Bb
Chi nna Ye . su Baa . lan Ma nnil
Van dha dhaa . le Ma gi may
Bb,F,D
Bb,F,D
F#
Bb
33
Bb Bb Bb Bb C A Bb F G
Bb Bb Bb Bb C A Bb
Ye nne Ye . nne pu dhu may Vi nnil
Ke ta Sei . dhi I ni may
Bb,F,D
Bb,F#,Db
Bb,F,D
35
Bb Bb Bb Bb C A Bb F G
Bb Bb Bb Bb C A Bb
Chi nna Ye . su Baa . lan Ma nnil
Van dha dhaa . le Ma gi may
Bb,F,D
Bb,F,D
Cm
F
Bb
37
D D D Eb D C A Bb C C C D C Bb C Db
Kan dhai Ko la thi le Pa su
Pu lla nin Man ja thi le Ye he
Bb,F,D
G,Eb,C
A,F,C
Bb,F,D
Cm
F
Bb
39
D D D F Eb D C D C A Bb C C C C F D C Bb
Kan dhai Ko . la thi le . . Pa su
Pu lla nin Man . ja thi le
Bb,F,D
G,Eb,C
A,F,C
Bb,F,D

Eb   F   Gm   Cm   Dm   Bb
41
G G A A A Bb Bb C C C   D D D Bb G G G A Bb C Bb
In draya Baa la nin Kan du Man dha yin   Me pe ru Ma yan dha na ve . . . .
Bb,G,Eb   A,F,C   Bb,G,D   G,Eb,C   A,F,D   Bb,F,D

F   Dm   Bb
43
F F F Bb A A A C Bb   F F F Eb D D   F F Bb A A A C Bb
A zha gi ya Vaa . nil . .   A dhi sa ya Raa gam .   Aa sa yil Koo . di . .

F   Dm   Eb   Bb
46
F F Eb D D   D Eb G G G Ab G F F F D D Eb
Thoo dha ri Koo tam .   A var Paa ti ni le O ru A dhi sa yam . A dhai

Eb   Bb   F   Bb
48
G G G Ab G F F F F   F G Bb C D   C D C Bb
Therin di run de Pu dhu Ra ga si yam .   U la gil Van dha .   Me . si ya . .

F   Bb   F#   Gm   Bb
51
C D C Bb   C D C Bb   C D C Bb
me . si ya .   Me . si ya .   Me . si ya . .

En Yesuve " G "

devotional

www.vp3.in whatsapp +91 8123235873

Transcribed By
Vp3 usc Music Notes & Karaoke

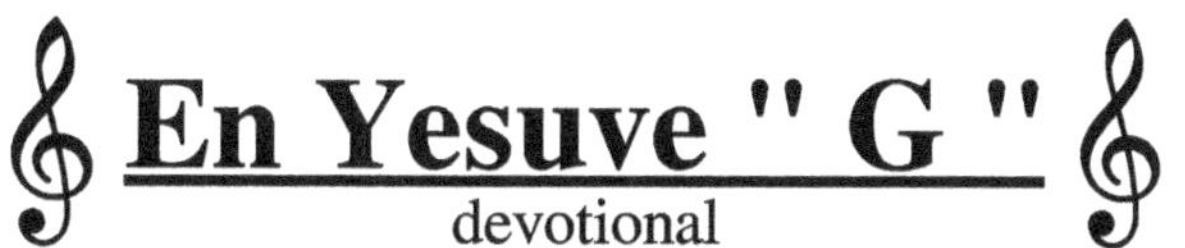

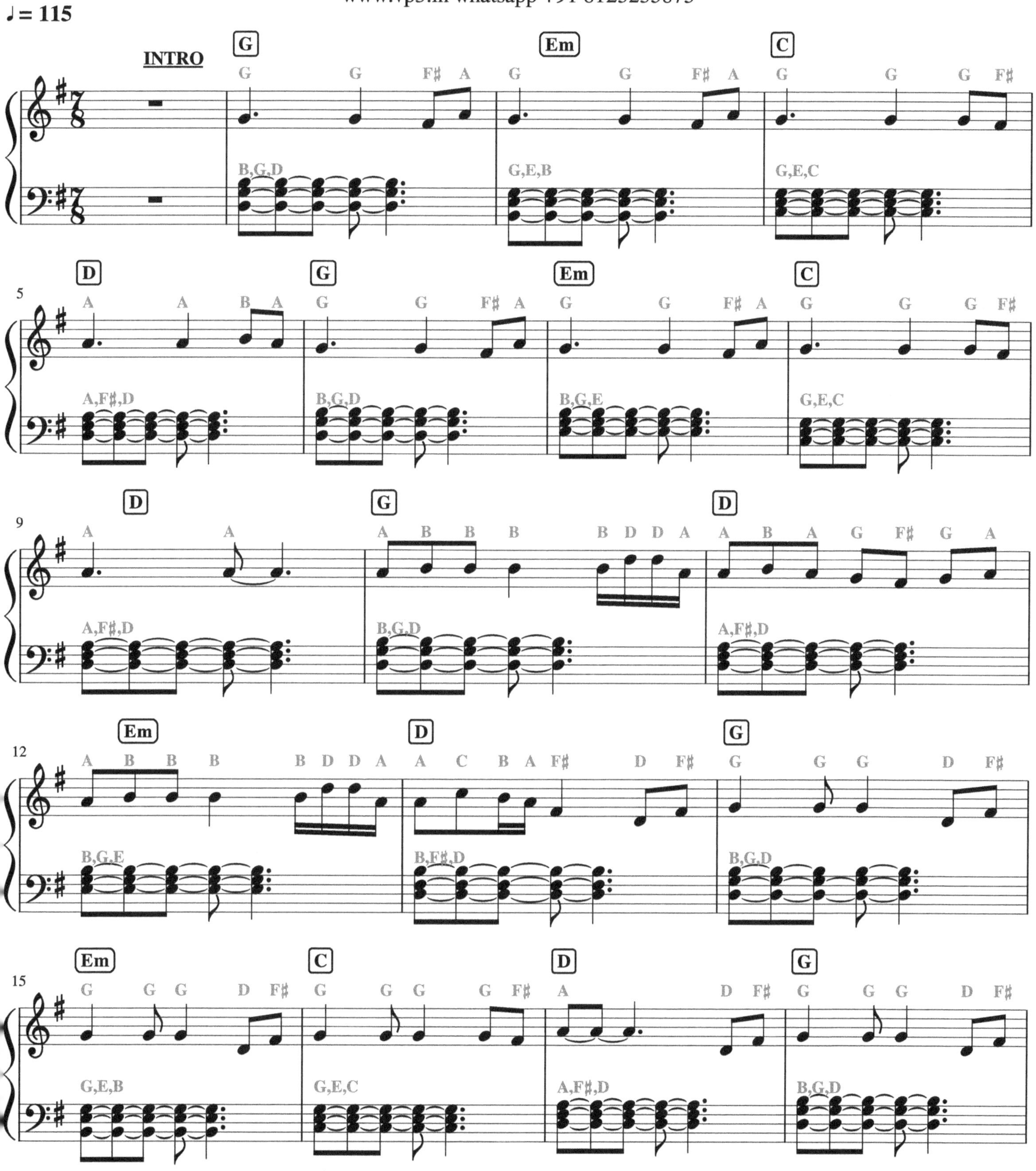

Em
C
D
G
D
C
D
G
G PALLAVI
Em+A
Am
D
G
Em+A
Am
D
C
Bm
En Ye su ve Na an U n tha n Pil lai
Paar vai ya na lum En na i Ye rk ka Ma rak ku vil
lai Um mai Ni nai th u Vaa zha vu m
2 En Yesuve

36
C
C C C C D E
Ummi l Ni lai th u
G,E,C
Bm
D D A B A B
Vaa zha vu m Aru l
F#,D,B
C
C C C B A
Pu ri yu m a e
G,E,C
39
D
A C B G F#
An ba r Ye su vae
A,F#,D
G
G
G,D,B
Em
G,E,B
C
C C C D E
Um mai Ni nai th a
G,E,C
43
Bm
D D A B
Vaa zh vu m
F#,D,B
C
C C C C D E
Um mil Ni lai th a
G,E,C
Bm
D D A B A B
Vaa zh vu m Aru l
F#,D,B
46
C
C C C C B A
Pu ri yu m a e
G,E,C
D
A C B G F#
An ba r Ye su ve
A,F#,D
G
G
G,D,B
Em
G,E,B
50
G
B A B A G F#
Pothu m A n ba e
B,G,D
D
D B A
Neer Po thu m
A,F#,D
Em
B B A B A G F#
U ma thu U ra vi l
B,G,E
3 En Yesuve

Bm
C
D
B
53
D D B A A E E E F# F# F# F# F# F#
Ni rai vu Ven dum Ummi l Ent rum Ni laik kum Va ram Thaa
B,F#,D G,E,C A,F#,D F#,D#,B

Em
D
G
D
56
G B A B A G F# D B A
ru m . . . . Pothu m A n ba e Neer Po thu m
G,E,B A,F#,D B,G,D A,F#,D

Em
Bm
C
60
B B A B A G F# D D B A A E E E E
U ma thu U ra vi l Ni rai vu Ven dum Ummi l En trum
B,G,E B,F#,D G,E,C

D
B
G
G
INTERLUDE - 1
G
C
63
F# F# F# F# F# F# G G F# E D
Ni laik kum Va ra Thaa ru m . . . .
A,F#,D F#,D#,B G,D,B G,D,B B,G,D G,E,C

Am
D
G
C
Am
D
G
Bm
Am
D
67
C A A D G F# E D C A A D D G F# D A G F# F# G
A,E,C A,F#,D B,G,D G,E,C A,E,C A,F#,D G,D,B F#,D,B A,E,C A,F#,D

Tha ro r a ro tha ra ro tha ra
thaa ro r a ro tha ra ro tha ra ra ra r a thara
raa ra r a tha ra raa ra ra ra ra ra a
B A G G A G F# F# E C F# F# G C B A G
CHARANAM
Ye su ve Um mai Ma rak kum bo thu Paa vam E n na i

Bm
89
F# G E D
Ne ruk ku the y
F#,D,B
G
D D D C D B C A A D D D
E thi lum U m m ai
G,D,B
D
Ni naik kum bo thu
A,F#,D
C
92
E E E E A G A
Si lu vai A n b u
G,E,C
Bm
F# G E D
Ni raik ku the y
F#,D,B
G
D D G G G F#
Un mai Ma ra v a
B,G,D
Am
95
F# A A A A
U nar vin Ul lam
A,E,C
D
F# G A A A D
Naa lum E nak k u
A,F#,D
Em
B A B A G
Thaa ru m a e
G,E,B
G
98
D D D G G F#
U ru thi ya U m
B,G,D
Am
F# A A A A A
U ra vil Va la ra
A,E,C
D
F# F# G A A A D C
I ru thi va ra y u m
A,F#,D
Bm
101
B B B B B C
U tha vu m a e
B,F#,D
C
C C C C A A F#
I ru thi va ra yu m
G,E,C
D
A,F#,D
D
F# D D G
U tha vu ma e
A,F#,D
G
B,G,D

G
104
B A B A G F#
Pothu m A n ba e
B,G,D
D
D B A
Nee r Po thum
A,F#,D
Em
B B A B A G F#
U ma thu U ra vi l
B,G,E
Bm
D D B A A
Ni rai vu Ven dam
B,F#,D
C
E E E E
Ummi l En trum
G,E,C
D
F# F# F# F# F# F#
Ni laik kum Va ram Thaa
A,F#,D
B
F#,D#,B
Em
107
110
G
ru m
G,E,B
D
A,F#,D
G
B A B A G F#
Pothu m A n ba e
B,G,D
D
113
D B A
Nee r Po thum
A,F#,D
Em
B B A B A G F#
U ma thu U ra vi l
B,G,E
Bm
D D B A A
Ni rai vu Ven dam
B,F#,D
C
116
E E E E
Ummi l En trum
G,E,C
D
F# F# F# F# F# F#
Ni laik kum Va ra Thaa
A,F#,D
B
F#,D#,B
G
G
ru m
G,D,B
7 En Yesuve

INTERLUDE - 2
119
G
G
Am
F
D D G F# A A
C B B A
G,D,B
G,D,B
A,E,C
A,F,C
123
D
G
Am
F
D D G F# A
D C B A A
A,F#,D
G,D,B
A,E,C
A,F,C
127
D
G
Bm
C
A B
G B A B B A G
G A G B A G F#
G F# E D
A,F#,D
G,E,B
F#,D,B
G,E,C
131
D
G
BM
C
A
G B A B B A G
G A G B A G F#
E E D E G F#A
A,F#,D
G,E,B
F#,D,B
G,E,C
whatsapp
+91 8123235873
135
G
G
G,D,B

Indru Namakaga " C "
prayer
www.vp3.in whatsapp +91 8123235873
Transcribed By
Vp3 Music Notes & Karaoke
♩ = 105
INTRO
C   C   C   C   C   C   C   C   C   E   D   C   C   B
Maan dhar A nai va ru .kkum . . Ma gi zh chi yoo . tum
D C B G B B C   C   C E D C C   C   C C B D C B G
. . . . Nar Sey dhi . . In dru Ka . ve ri Oo ri le . . . . .
B C E G B C   B   B   B B   C B   C
. . Meet . . . . par . Pi ran dhu . llar .
C BIT MUSIC
C B C D E D C B C B C D E D C B C D E D E G E G B G B C B G E D
G,E,C
G,E,C
C B C D E D C B C B C D E D C B C D E D E G E G B G B C B G E D
G,E,C
G,E,C
13

G
Em
C
PALLAVI
C
In dru Na ma . kka . ga . Meet . par Pi ran . du .
G
Em
G
C
llar . . . A va re . Aan . da var Me si ya . . In dru Na ma ka . . ga .
G
Em
G
C
. Meet . par Pi ra . du . llar . . . A va re . Aan . da var Me si ya . . . .
INTERLUDE - 1
Em
G
Em
2 Indru Namakkaga

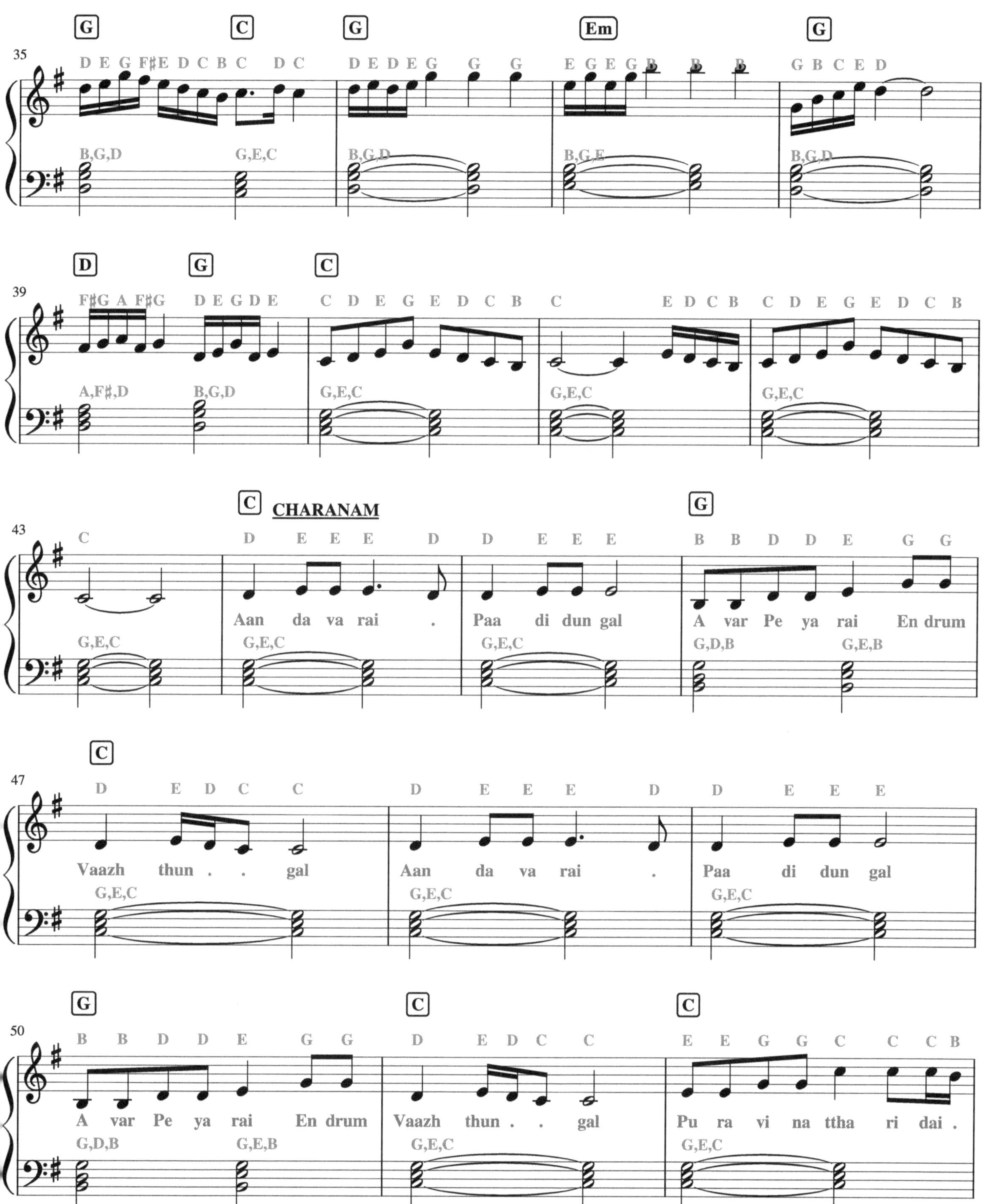

CHARANAM
Aan da va rai . Paa di dun gal
A var Pe ya rai En drum
Vaazh thun . . gal
Aan da va rai . Paa di dun gal
A var Pe ya rai En drum Vaazh thun . . gal
Pu ra vi na ttha ri dai .

A va ra . dhu Mat chi yam E du tthu So . llun . . gal .
Pu ra vi na ttha ri dai. A va ra . dhu Mat chi yam E du tthu So . llun . .
gal . Nee . dhi . . yu dan A var Poo . va zha gai . . . .
Aat . chi Se . var E na . A ri yun . . gal Nee . dhi . . yu dan A var
Poo . va zha gai . . . . Aat . chi Se . var E na . A ri yun . . gal In dru

68
G G G B D C G C B G B G E D E G E
Na ma kka . ga . Meet . par Pi ran . du . llar . .
G,E,C G,E,C G,E,C
G Em G C
71
B B D D E E G G D D G E D C E F G G B B D D C
A va re . Am . da var Me si . ya . var In dru Na ma kka . . ga .
G,D,B G,E,B G,D,B G,E,C G,E,C
G Em G C
74
G C B G B G E D E G E B B D D E G G D D E D C C
. Ye . su Pi ran . du . llar . . . A va re . Aan . da var Me si ya . . .
G,E,C G,E,C G,D,B G,E,B G,D,B G,E,C
INTERLUDE - 2
G Em
78
E D C B G C D C B G E G
G,E,C G,E,C B,G,D B,G,E
G Em C
86
D D D E E E G G G B B B B C C C C C C C C C C C C C C C C C C C C C
B,G,D B,G,E G,E,C

Jayitthuvittar " C "
christian song
www.vp3.in whatsapp +91 8123235873
Transcribed By
Vp3 Music Notes & Karaoke
= 110
INTRO
Je yi thu Vi tt ar Ma ra na thai
Vi zhun gi Vi tt ar Saa vi nai
Ezhu n du Vi tt ar Jee va noa dae .
Ven ru Vi tt ar Paa va thai
Kon ru Vi tt ar Saa ba thai
Vyi r thu Vi tt ar En ren ru mae .
Kon da a du vom

INTERLUDE - 1
CHARANAM - 1
Kon da a du vom
Vyi ru da n Ezhun tha va rai
Kon da a du vom
Kon da a du vom
Kon da a du vom
Vyi ru da n Ezhun tha va rai
Kon da a du vom
O di thu vi tt ar Saa vin soo r
Je yi thu Vi tt ar Nara ga thai
Mu di thu Vi tt ar Ki ri yai thaa nai
www.vp3.in
info.vp3@gmail.com
2 Jayatthuvittar

19

3 Jayatthuvittar

CHARANAM - 2
61
E E D C C   G A C
A r pa ri th u Aa du voa m
E E D C C   G A C
Maga zh thi yo da e Paa du vom
G,E,C
G,E,C

Dm   G   F   C
63
F F F F F   D E F G F
Ye s u En rr um Jee vi kki raar .
E D C C   G A C
En gum sel voa m Nar sei di
A,F,D   B,G,D A,F,C
G,E,C

Dm   G   C   Am
66
E D C C   G A C
Kon du sel voa m Savi se sham
F F F F F   D E F
Ye s u Naa ma m Paat ri du voam .
G   C B G A
Kon da a du vom
G,E,C   A,F,D   B,G,D   G,E,C   A,E,C

G   Em F   Dm   G   C   Am
70
B C D G   F F F F D D D E F   G E D C   C B G A
Kon da a du vom   Vyi ru da n Ezhun tha va rai   Kon da a du vom   Kon da a du vom
B,G,D B,G,E A,F,C   A,F,D B,G,D G,E,C G,E,C A,E,C

G   Em F   Dm   G   C
74
B C D G   F F F F D D D E F   G E D C
Kon da a du vom   Vyi ru da n Ezhun tha va rai   Kon da a du vom
B,G,D B,G,E A,F,C   A,F,D B,G,D G,E,C

4 Jayatthuvittar

Jillena Kulirkatru " A "
devotional
www.vp3.in whatsapp +91 8123235873
Music : Isaac Dharmakumar
Transcribed By
Vp3 Music Notes & Karaoke
= 133
INTRO
PALLAVI
Ji lla na Ku lir Kaa tru Vee sum Ne ra mi dhu
ME lo . ga Thoo dhar . Koo ttam Paa dum Ve la ya dhu Ma nnin Maa . da ram .
22

Kadharam Ne ra madhu Nam Me si ya MAnnil U dhi ttha r .
Ji lla na Ku lir Kaa tru Vee sum Ne ra midhu ME lo . ga Thoodhar . Koo ttam
Paa dum Ve la yadhu Ma nnin Maa . da ram . Kadharam Ne ra madhu Nam
Me si ya MAnnil U dhi ttha r . Nat cha thi ra Naduvaa nil O li Vi la kkay .
Saas tri gal Pin Tho darnda re . . . . . . Ve llai Po lam Thoo ba var kkum

3 Jillena Kulirkatru

E
Bm
E
D
E
56
B
B C# D C# B
A A A B C# B
nar . MAn dahi MEy ppar gal . . Pu dhu Gaa nam Paa di ye .
EG#,B,
DF#,B,
EG#,B,
DF#,A,
EG#,B,

Bm
E
D
E
A
E
61
B C# D C# B C# B B A F# A B C# B C# C# C# B B B B C#
Vin dahi Kaa na ve . . . . Vi ran dho di Sen dra nar . Ji lla na Ku lir Kaa tru
DF#,B,
EG#,B,
DF#,A,
EG#,B,
C#E,A, BE,G#, F#A,C#,E,

F#m7
A
D
66
C# C# C# B B B A A A A A B
. . Ji lla na Ku lir Kaa tru Vee sum Ne ra mi dhu
AC#,E,
AD,F#,

F#m
E
A
69
C# C# E B C# B A F# A A A F# E C# C# B B B A
ME lo . ga Thoo dhar . Koo ttam Paa dum Ve la ya dhu Ma nnin Maa . da ram .
AC#,F#,
G#B,E,
AC#,E,

D
A
72
A A A A A A B C# D D D B C# B A A A
Ka dha ram Ne ra ma dhu Nam Me si ya MAnnil U dhi ttha r .
AD,F#,
DF#,A,
EA,C#,
whatsapp +91 8123235873

4 Jillena Kulirkatru

A
D
F#m
75
C# C# C# B B B A   A A A A A B   C# C# E B C# B A F#
Ji lla na Ku lir Kaa tru   Vee sum Ne ra mi dhu   ME lo . ga Thoodhar . Koo ttam
AC#,E,   AD,F#,   AC#,F#,

E
A
D
78
A A A A F# E   C# C# B B B A   A A A A A B   C#
Paa dum Ve la ya dhu   Ma nnin Maa . da ram .   Kadharam Ne ra madhu   Nam
G#B,E,   AC#,E,   AD,F#,
info.vp3@gmail.com

A
A POSTLUDE
D
81
D D D B C# B A A   A   A A A A B B B BA   A A A D C# B A
Me si ya MAnnil U dhi ttha   r .
DF#,A,   EA,C#,   C#,E,A,   DF#,A,

F#m
D
A
D
85
A A A A B B B BA   A A A E D C# A   A A A A B B B BA   A A A D C# B A
C#F#,A,   DF#,A,   C#,E,A,   DF#,A,

F#m
D
89
A A A A B B B BA   A A A E D C# A
C#F#,A,   DF#,A,

5 Jillena Kulirkatru

Mannil Vantha "G "

ma jaikumar

www.vp3.in whatsapp +91 8123235873

Music : MA Jaikumar

♩ = 155

G   Bm   C   D
40
D C C B   B B D   D B A   B A B   E C B   C B C   F# D C#
Po ran dha va   rae . .   Ma zhai yi   l a e   Pa ni yi   l a e   Ku li ri
B,G,D   www.vp3.in   B,F#,D   C,C,E   A,F#,D

G   Bm   Am   G   C
47
D   D C C B   B B B   B D B   A C A   G B A   G F# E
lae   Po ran dha va   rae Un nai   Vaa zh thu   Va nan gi   Pu gal vo   mae . .
B,G,D   B,F#,D   A,E,C   B,G,D   G,E,C

INTERLUDE - 1
G   Em   Bm   D
54
D B A   B   B C D   B A G   B   D E F# G A B
Man nil Van   dha   Nin na yi   l a e .   .
B,G,D   B,G,E   B,F#,D   A,F#,D

G   C   G   Bm   Am   D
62
D G F# G E D   B G F# G   D G F# G E G   B A G   A   A   B
B,G,D   G,E,C   B,G,D   B,F#,D   A,E,C   A,F#,D

Em   C   D   CHARANAM   G
71
A F# D E   G F# D B   C E D B G   A D C#   D C B   B D D
Ka n gal
A,F#,D   B,G,E   G,E,C   G,E,C   A,F#,D   B,G,D

Em G Em D7 D C
Thoo n ga Vi n gal ya a ga Van dha . De v a Paa la ka nae
G Em G Em D7
Kan g al Thoo n ga Vi n g a l ya a ga Van dha . De v a
D C G Am
Paa la ka nae Vi di gaa la A ru ga e Va zhi Kaat tu Ma ra vae
C D Bm G
Mi nna l Va zhi yaa ga Vandh a va rae Vi di gaa la A ru ga e
Am C D
Va zhi Kaat tu Ma ra vae Min na l Va zhi yaa ga Van dh a va
info.vp3@gmail.com
whatsapp
+91 8123235873

Bm   Am   G   C   G
109
B B B B D B A C A G B A G F# E D B A
nae Un nai Vaa zh thu Va nan gi Pugazh v o mae . . Man nil Van
B,F#,D B,F#,D A,E,C B,G,D G,E,C B,G,D

Em   C   Em   D
115
B B C D B A G G G A G F# E E E G E D
dha Nin na yi lae . . Mu rai yil Ma di yil Nin da a va rae
B,G,E G,E,C B,G,E A,F#,D

G   Em   Bm   G INTERLUDE - 2
122
D B A B B C D B A G B B G
Man nil Van dha Nin na yi l a e . .
B,G,D B,G,E B,F#,D B,G,D

D   G   C   D   C
130
E E D B G E D F# E D E D C C D
A,F#,D B,G,D G,E,C A,F#,D G,E,C

Bm   D   D G
139
C B B C B A D E F# G
B,F#,D A,F#,D A,F#,D B,G,D

Margazhi Poove " D "
christian devotional
www.vp3.in whatsapp +91 8123235873
Transcribed By
Vp3 Music Notes & Karaoke
♩ = 117
INTRO
PALLAVI
Mar ga zhi Poo ve . Mar ga zhi Poo ve Ma zha lai Mo zhi Pe sa va .

31

Gm   C   Bb
G G A Bb A G A F# E E F# G F# E F#E D D C C C Bb Bb D C
I rul Sool . U la gil . . O li vi la kka . ga . . An . da van Thon . dra .
Bb,G,D   G,E,C   Bb,F,D

D   D   Gm   D
D A,F#G,E D F# G A A G Bb Bb D A A G G A F# F# F# G A
va Mar ga zhi Poo ve . Mar ga zhi Poo ve Ma zha lai Mo zhi Pe sa va .
A,F#,D   A,F#,D   Bb,G,D   Bb,G,D   A,F#,D
G,E F#,D

Gm   C   Bb
G G A Bb A G A F# E E F# G F# E F#E D D C C C Bb Bb D C
I rul Sool . U la gil . . O li vi la kka . ga . . An . da van Thon . dra .
Bb,G,D   G,E,C   Bb,F,D

D   D   C   D   D   C
D D D C C C D D F# E D D D D C C C C D F#
va . Ye . la yil Nee pi . ra . kka . Va san dhan gal Vaa .zh vil .
A,F#,D   A,F#,D   G,E,C   A,F#,D   A,F#,D   G,E,C

D   C   D   Gm
F# F# E D D C C C D C Bb Bb A G A A G G A Bb A G A F#
Koo di va . ra Ye . nna . . Tha . vam Naan Sei dhen . Kan . ma ni Po . le . .
A,F#,D   G,E,C   A,F#,D   Bb,G,D

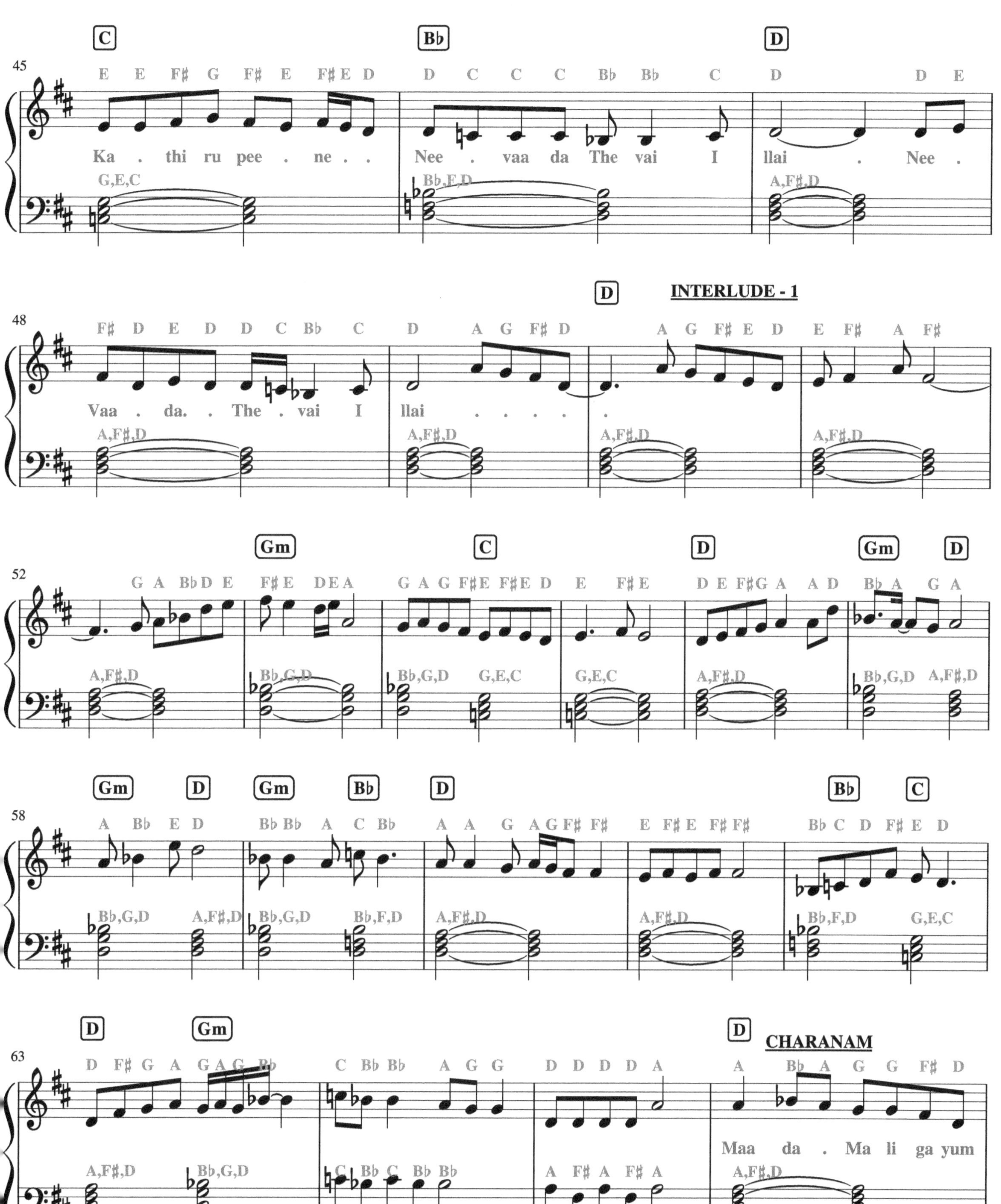

INTERLUDE - 1
CHARANAM
Ka . thi ru pee . ne . . Nee . vaa da The vai I llai . Nee .
Vaa . da. . The . vai I llai . . . .
Maa da . Ma li ga yum
3 Margazhi Poove

BIT MUSIC
U na kku I llai   Maa ttu Tho lu va me .   Nee . Thern . dhai
Pan ju Mettha . yo .   U na kku I llai   Pa su mai Tha li ra ye .   Nee . Kon . dai
Maa da . Ma li ga yum   U na kku I llai
Maa ttu Tho lu va me .   Nee . Ther n dha .   Pan ju Mettha . yo .   U na kku I llai
Pa su mai Tha li ra ye .   Nee . . Kon . dai   Pi dhu Mo zhi Sin dhum .
4 Margazhi Poove

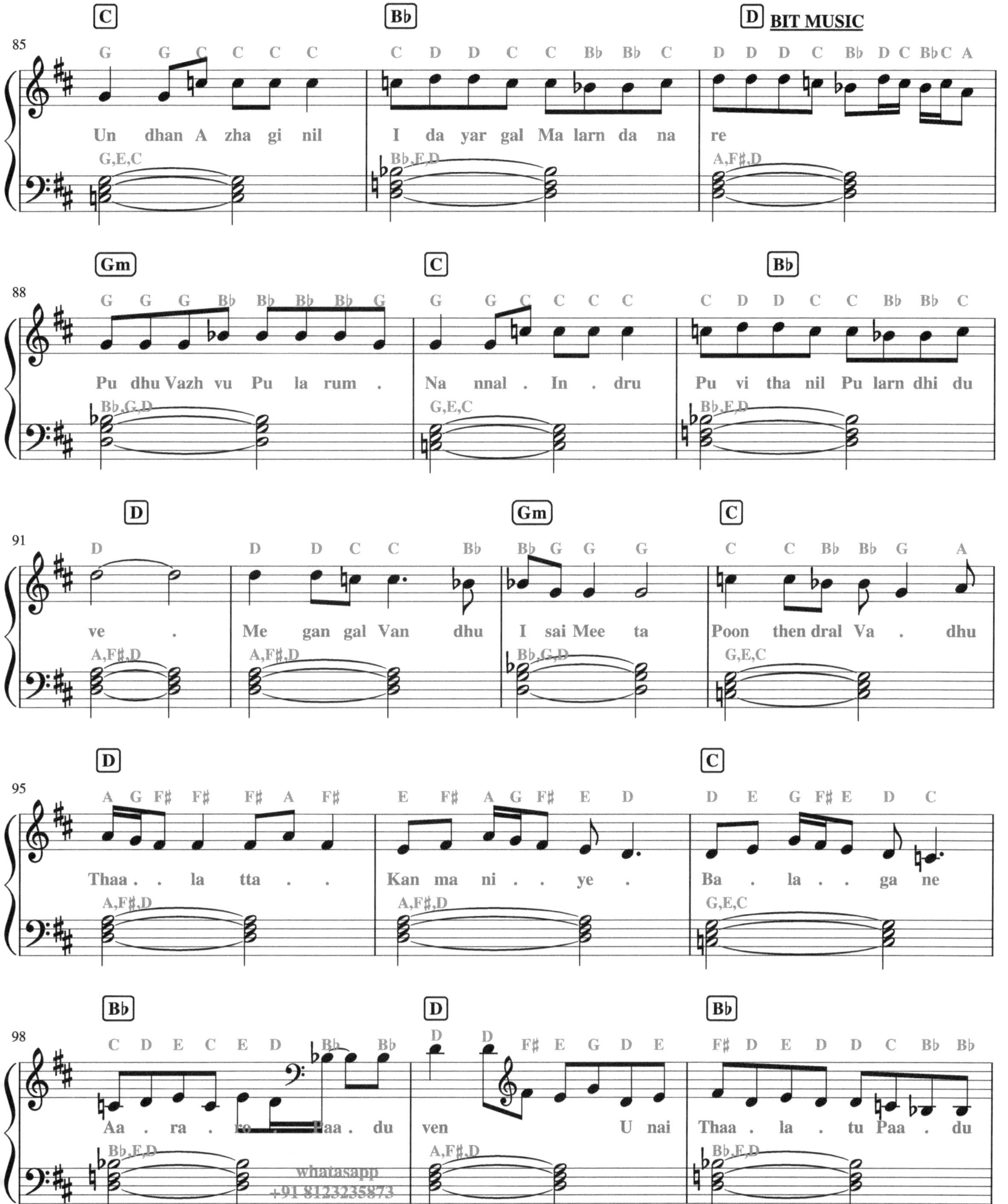
BIT MUSIC
5 Margazhi Poove
whatasapp
+91 8123235873
Un dhan A zha gi nil
I da yar gal Ma larn da na re
Pu dhu Vazh vu Pu la rum .
Na nnal . In . dru
Pu vi tha nil Pu larn dhi du
ve .
Me gan gal Van dhu
I sai Mee ta
Poon then dral Va . dhu
Thaa . . la tta . .
Kan ma ni . . ye .
Ba . la . . ga ne
Aa . ra . ko Haa . du ven
U nai Thaa . la . tu Paa . du

INTERLUDE - 2
www.vp3.in
infovp3@gmail.com
6 Margazhi Poove

Meetpar Pirandhullar " C "
prayer
www.vp3.in whatsapp +91 8123235873
Transcribed By
Vp3 Music Notes & Karaoke
= 110
INTRO
Dm
Bb
Dm
F
Dm
D C D   D E F E D   D C D   F G A G F E D
A,F,D   Bb,F,D   A,F,D   A,F,C   A,F,D
A
Dm
Bb
D D A D D A   E E A E E A   D D A D D   F E D   E F G A A
A,F,D   A,E,C#   A,F,D   Bb,F,D
Dm
PALLAVI
Bb
C
Dm
A   A A G F E   D E F E D E C D   A A A A G F E
Meet par Pi ran dhu llar   A va re . Me si ya .   . Ma gizhn dhu Paa . di .
A,F,D   Bb,F,D   G,E,C   A,F,D
Bb
Dm
Bb
C
D E F E D   A   A A G F E   D E F E D E C D
Aa r pa ri ppom   . Meet par Pi ran dhu llar   A va re . Me si ya .
Bb,F,D   A,F,D   A,F,D   Bb,F,D   G,E,C
Dm
Bb
Dm
F
Gm
A A A A G F E   D E F E D DE   F G F A A G DE
. Ma gizhn dhu Paa . di .   Aa r pa ri ppom Nam .   Meet parum A va re   Nal .
A,F,D   Bb,F,D   A,F,D   A,F,C   Bb,G,D
37

Me parum A va re Nam.
Meet parum A va re Nal.
Mey pparum A va re
. I nni sai Mu zhan gi da
Chirt . mas Pi ran dha dhe
. Meet par Pi ran dhu llar
A va re . Me si ya .
. Ma gizhn dhu Paa . di .
Aa r pa ri ppom
INTERLUDE - 1
info.vp3@gmail.com
www.vp3.in
2 Meetpar Pirandhulla

CHARANAM
An . da var Ye . su . An bai Tha ra Van dhar
Amn . Mee dhu Tha vazhn dhi da Maa da dai yil Pi ran dhar A ru lai Po zhin dhi da
A ga I ru lai A gar thi da . Ma . . nu dan Paa . va thai Po . ka ve Van dhar
A ru lai Po zhin dhi da A ga I ru lai A gar thi da . Ma . . nu dan Paa . va thai
Po . ka ve Van dhar Ma gizh vom . . Pu gazh vom . . .

INTERLUDE - 2
Ma nno rai Rat cha ka rai .
Meet par Pi ran dhu llar
A va re . Me si ya .
. Ma gizhn dhu Paa . di . Aa r pa ri ppom
4 Meetpar Pirandhulla

Nalliravil Vandhudhitthe " Dm "

christian devotional (munnaniyile)
www.vp3.in whatsapp +91 8123235873

Music : Ivan Jeevaraj

Transcribed By
Vp3 Music Notes & Karaoke

Gm   F   E   A7
19
G A G G Bb A F F   Ab   Ab Ab Ab   A
Ye . nnai Meet kka Pi ran dha   Vaa   sa Ma   la   re
Bb,G,D   A,F,C   B,Ab,E   A,G,E,C#

Dm   Fm   Bb   F   Dm   Gm
21
A A A F G F E D   D E F G A   D A A F G F E D
Na lli ra vil Van dhu dhi ttha   Vi nnin Jo thi ye   Pu lla nai yil Ma larn dhi tta
A,F,D   Bb,G,D   Bb,F,D   A,F,C   A,F,D   Bb,G,D

INTERLUDE - 1

Bb   F   C   Am   Bb   F   C   F
24
D E F G A   E C A   A G E F G A   E C A A C Bb A
De va Main dha ne
Bb,F,D   A,F,C   G,E,C   A,E,C   Bb,F,D   A,F,C   G,E,C   A,F,C

Bb   A7   DmAdd11   Bb   C7
28
BbA Bb G A   E   D E F E D C   B Bb   G F E F G Ab
Bb,F,D   A,G,E,C#   A,G,E,D   Bb,E,D   Bb,G,E,C

Dm   Gm   Dm   D   A7
32
A   Bb A G A Bb D A G F   F# G E F# G   C# A
A,F,D   Bb,G,D   A,F,D   A,F#,D   A,G,E,C#

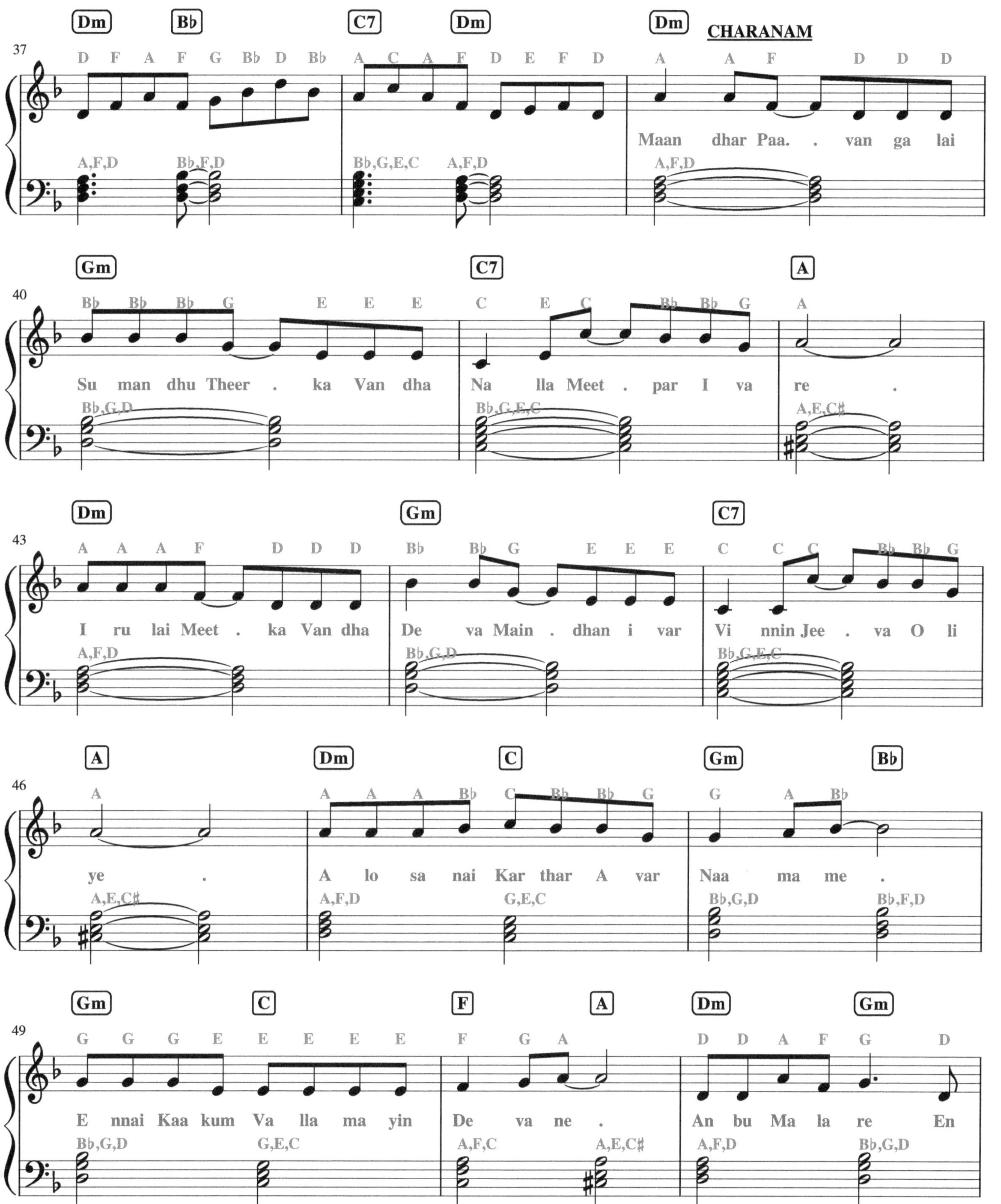

CHARANAM
Maan dhar Paa. van ga lai
Su man dhu Theer . ka Van dha
Na lla Meet . par I va re .
I ru lai Meet . ka Van dha
De va Main . dhan i var
Vi nnin Jee . va O li
ye . A lo sa nai Kar thar A var
Naa ma me .
E nnai Kaa kum Va lla ma yin
De va ne . An bu Ma la re En
3 Nalliravil Vandhu
43

Dm Gm Dm Gm Bb A7
52
Vaa sa Ma la re A nnai Ma di yil De va Paa la ne
A,F,D Bb,G,D A,F,D Bb,G,D Bb,F,D A,G,E,C#

Dm Fm Bb F Dm Gm
55
Na lli ra vil Van dhu dhi ttha Vi nnin Jo thi ye Pu lla nai yil Ma larn dhi tta
A,F,D Bb,G,D Bb,F,D A,F,C A,F,D Bb,G,D

Bb F Dm C7 Bb Gm
58
De va Main dha ne Vi nna va rum Ma . nna va rum Ma giln dhi na re
Bb,F,D A,F,C A,F,D Bb,G,E,C Bb,F,D Bb,G,D

Gm F E A7
61
Ye . nnai Meet kka Pi ran dha Vaa sa Ma la re
Bb,G,D A,F,C B,Ab,E A,G,E,C#

Dm Fm Bb F Dm Gm
63
Na lli ra vil Van dhu dhi ttha Vi nnin Jo thi ye Pu lla nai yil Ma larn dhi tta
A,F,D Bb,G,D Bb,F,D A,F,C A,F,D Bb,G,D

4 Nalliravil Vandhu

INTERLUDE - 2
De va Main dha ne
C7
info.vp3@gmail.com
whatsapp
+91 8123235873
5 Nalliravil Vandhu
45

Music : Benny John Joseph

Transcribed By
Vp3 Music Notes & Karaoke

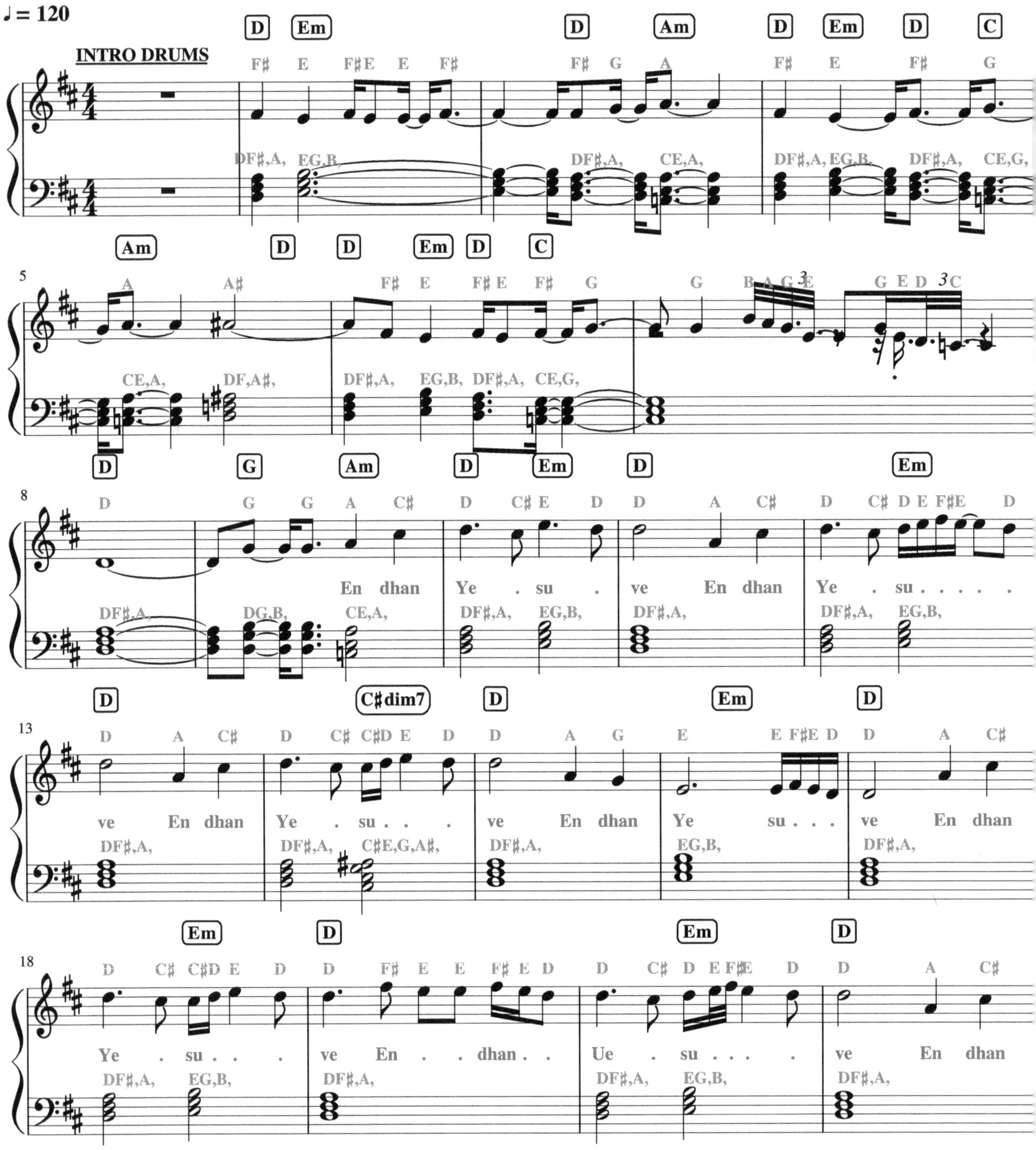

♩ = 120

INTRO DRUMS

46

C#dim7
D
Em
D
Ye . su . . . ve En dhan Ye su . . ve
DF#,A, C#E,G,A#, DF#,A, EG,B, DF#,A,
Em
D
Em D STANZA - 1
Paa van . gal Po kka . ve
EG,B, DF#,A,
Saa ban . gal Nee kka . ve Boo lo . gam Van dha . ra yya
DF#,A, DF#,A, DF#,A,
ma ni dha . nai Meet ka . ve Pa ra lo . gam Thi ra kka . ve
DF#,A, DF#,A,
Si lu va . yai Su man dha . ra yya Paa van . gal Po kka . ve
DF#,A, DF#,A, DF#,A,

38
F# F# E E D E
F# F# E G G F# F#
Saa ban . gal Nee kka . ve
Boo lo . gam Van dhaa . ra yya
DF#,A,
DF#,A,
DF#,A,

41
F# F# F# E G G F#
F# F# F# E E D E
Ma ni dha . nai Meet ka . ve
Pa ra lo . gam Thi ra kka . ve
DF#,A,
DF#,A,

Em
43
F# F# F# E G G F# F#
A A D A
B B B B C C B A
Si lu vai yai Sum na dhaa . ra
yya Ka nnee rai .
Thu da thaa . ra . . .
DF#,A,
DF#,A,
EG,B,

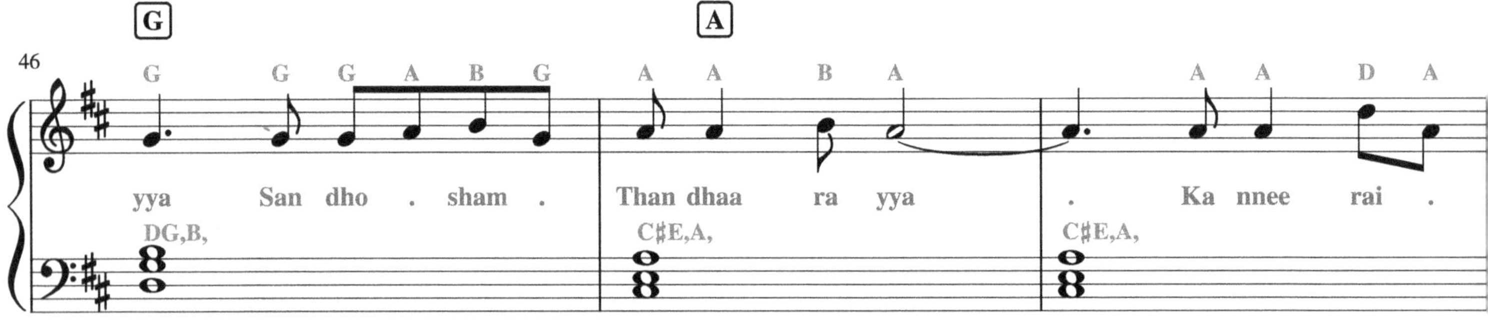
G
A
46
G G G A B G
A A B A
A A D A
yya San dho . sham .
Than dhaa ra yya
. Ka nnee rai .
DG,B,
C#E,A,
C#E,A,

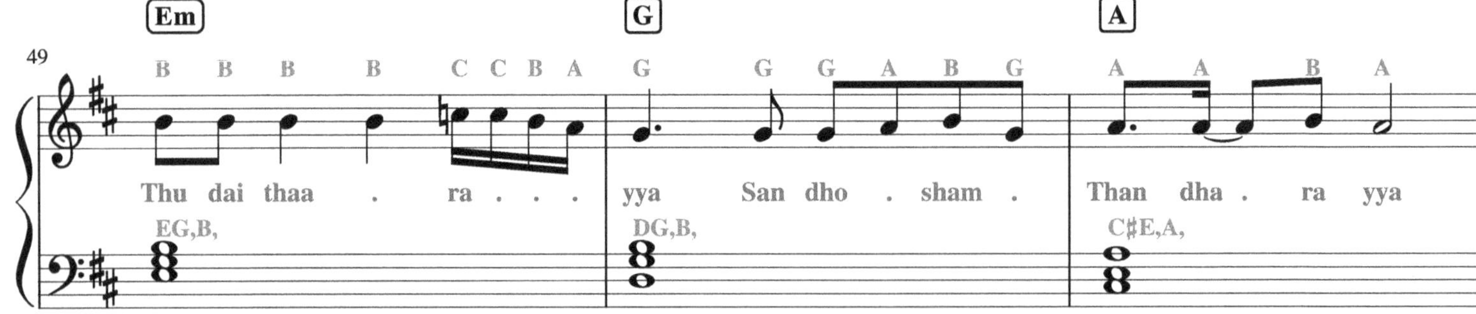
Em
G
A
49
B B B B C C B A G
G G A B G
A A B A
Thu dai thaa . ra . . .
yya San dho . sham .
Than dha . ra yya
EG,B,
DG,B,
C#E,A,

INTERLUDE 1
www.vp3.in
whatsapp +91 8123235873
4 Pavangal Pokkave

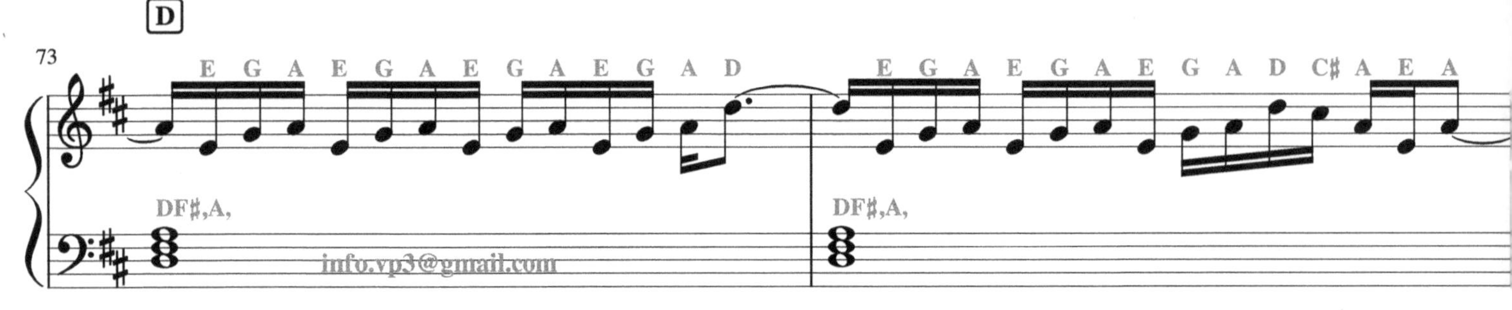
D
73
E G A E G A E G A E G A D
E G A E G A E G A D C# A E A
DF#,A,
info.vp3@gmail.com
DF#,A,

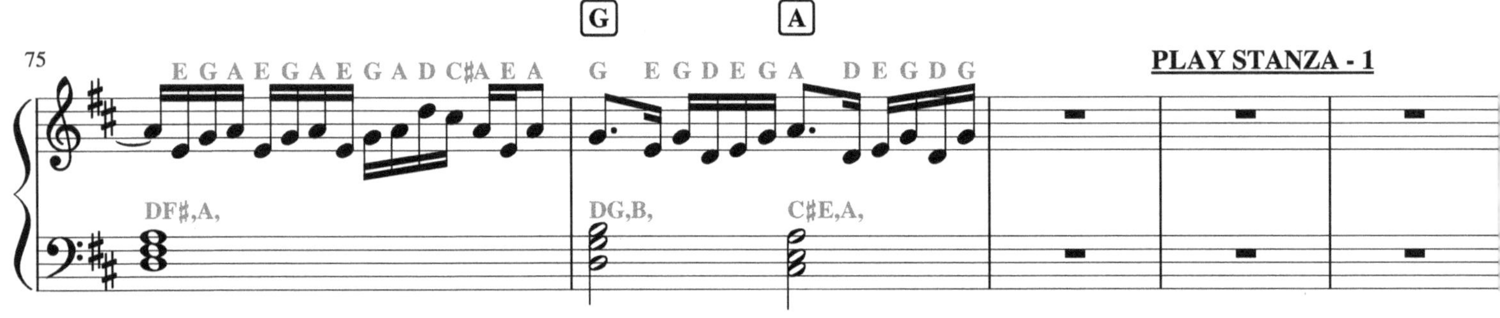
G
A
PLAY STANZA - 1
75
E G A E G A E G A D C# A E A
G E G D E G A D E G D G
DF#,A,
DG,B,
C#E,A,

D
INTERLUDE - 2
G
Bm
80
G F# E A
B A F# E D B
B A F# E D E F#G
B A F# E E D B
DF#,A,
DF#,A,
DG,B,
DF#,B,

A
D
G
BM
D
85
A B D D E F#E D
D E F#E D D E F#E D
D E F#E D D A B
C#E,A,
DF#,A,
DG,B,
DF#,B,
DF#,A,

Gm
D
G
A
PLAY STANZA - 1
88
D D E F#E D D E F#E D
G A G F# E F#E D
DG,A#,
DF#,A,
DG,B,
C#E,A,

D   POSTLUDE

94
E F# E D E D B D B A B A F# A F# E   F# E D E D B D B A B A F# A F# E D
DF#,A,   DF#,A,
whatsapp +91 8123235873

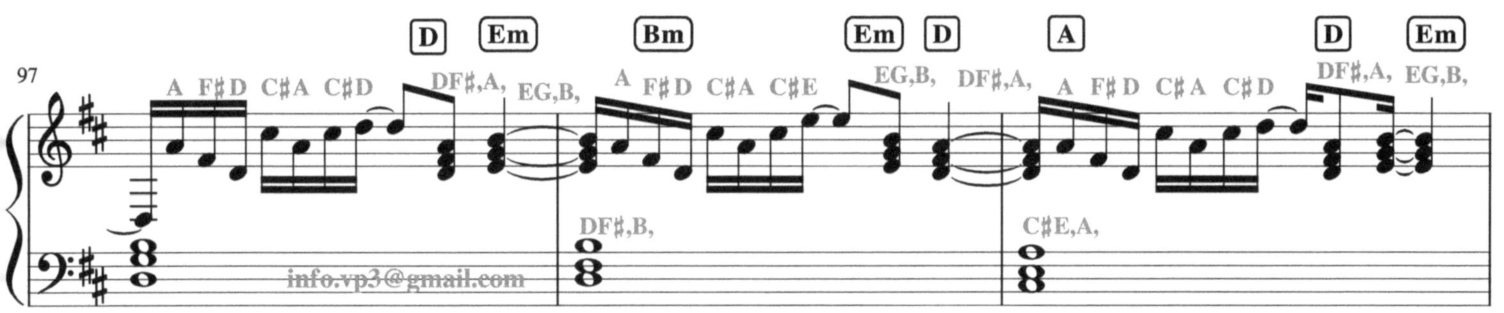

D   Em   Bm   Em D   A   D   Em
97
A F# D C# A C# D   DF#,A, EG,B,   A F# D C# A C# E   EG,B, DF#,A,   A F# D C# A C# D   DF#,A, EG,B,
DF#,B,   C#E,A,
info.vp3@gmail.com

100
C# A E B G D F# D A E C# A D B G E   D   C   D   B   A

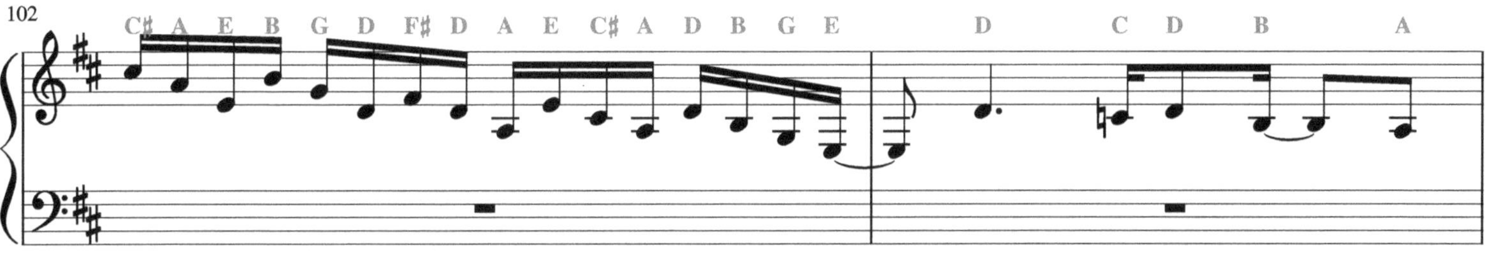

102
C# A E B G D F# D A E C# A D B G E   D   C   D   B   A

104
C# A E B   A E C# A A F# C# B   A

Panivilum Iravilum " D "
devotional
www.vp3.in whatsapp +91 8123235873
Transcribed By
Vp3 Music Notes & Karaoke
= 125
INTRO
Pa ni vizhum I ra vi nil Ye su . Mannil MA ni tha nay I rai ma gan Ye su .
PALLAVI
52

PA ni vi zhum I ra vi nil Ye su . Ma nnil Ma ni dha nay I rai ma gan
Ye su . Vaa na . thil Vin thoo . . . thar Paa da . An dha
Kaa na . thil Vin meen . . gal Aa da . . . . Pa ni vi zhum I ra vi nil
Ye su . Ma nnil MA ni tha nay I rai ma gan Ye su .
INTERLUDE - 1
info.vp3@gmail.com
whatsapp
+91 8123235873
2 Panivilum Iravilum

CHARANAM
Ka ni. vaa . . ga Ma nnoru . . Paa da . Engum
Ku lir Vaa . . dai I dha . ma . . ga Vee su . Su ga mma . na Raa ,3gan . gal;
Se . ra . O . di Vaa . . Then . dra le . . . . . .
3 Panivilum Iravilum

Ka ni . vaa . . ga Ma nno . . rum Paa da . EN GUM
Ku lir Vaa . . dai I dha ma ma . . ga Vee su .
Su ga maa . na Raa gan . . gal Se r . . . . . O . DI VAA . . Then . dra
le . . . . . . Ma la re Ma la re Ma larn dhi du . Ma gi zhum . MA na me
Than thi du . Ma la re Ma la re Ma larn dhi du . Ma gi zhum . Ma na me

INTERLUDE - 2
5 Panivilum Iravilum

Puthham Pudhu " D "
easter song
www.vp3.in whatsapp +91 8123235873
Transcribed By
Vp3 Music Notes & Karaoke

PALLAVI

G

20
D F# D F# A C# F#   D C# B C# B A G F#   G G G A B D G   B G B D B
Puttham Pu dhu Vaa . nam   Aa . . . . . .   Puttham Pu dhu Bhoo . mi   Aa . . . .
DF#,A,   DF#,A,   DG,B,   DG,B,

D   G   A   Em   F#m   D

24
A B A A A   A G   G A B A G F#E   C# D E A G F# E   E G F#E D C# D
Pu larndhadhu In dru .   Ye su . vi le . .   Ma larndhadhu In . dru   Vaa . zh vi ni . le
DF#,A,   DG,B,   C#E,A,   BE,G,   C#F#,A,   DF#,A,

D   G   A   Em   F#m   D

28
A B A A A   A G   G A B A G F#E   C# D E A G F# E   E G F#E D C# D
Pu larndhadhu In dru .   Ye su . vi le . .   Ma larndhadhu In . dru   Vaa . zh vi ni . le
A   D   E   F# G   C#   D E   F#   E D

D   G   A   D

32
F# A F# A A A   A B A B A G   G B G B B B   B C# B C# B A
Ha lle . lu ja Ha lle   Ha lle . . lu ja   Ha lle . lu ja Ha lle   Ha lle . . lu ja
D F# D F# F# F#   F#G F#G F# E   E G E G G G   G A G A G F#

D   G   A   D

36
F# A F# A A A   A B A B A G   G B G B B B   B C# B C# B A
Ha lle . lu ja Ha lle   Ha lle . . lu ja   Ha lle . lu ja Ha lle   Ha lle . . lu ja
D F# D F# F# F#   F#G F#G F# E   E G E G G G   G A G A G F#

2 Puttham Pudhu

D
INTERLUDE 1
40
www.vp3.in

C#m
C
D
44

Em
D
48
whatsapp +91 8123235873
info.vp3@gmail.com

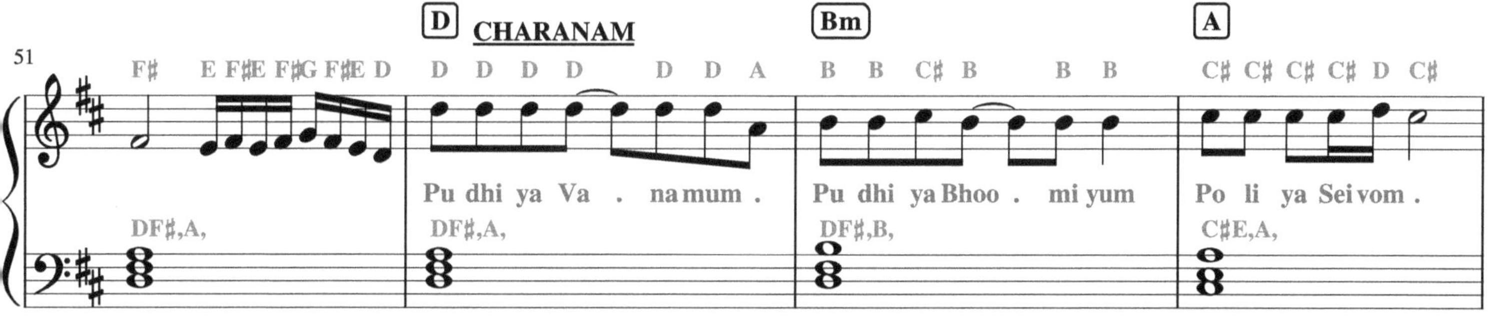
D   CHARANAM
Bm
A
51
Pu dhi ya Va . na mum .
Pu dhi ya Bhoo . mi yum
Po li ya Sei vom .

D
BIT MUSIC
55
Po li ya Sei vom

58
D Bm A D
D D D D D D A B B C# B B B C# C# C# C# D C# A G A G F#
Pu dhi ya Va . na mum . Pu dhi ya Bhoo . mi yum Po li ya Sei vom . Po li ya Sei vom
DF#,A, DF#,B, C#E,A, DF#,A,

62
G A D
F# A D D B B A A G F# E A A A A F# G B A A
Por ka . la Sin . dha . nai gal . U nnil Vi zhi ra Sei vom Vi zhi ra Sei vom
DF#,A, BD,G, C#E,A, DF#,A,

66
Bm A D
D E F# G B G B B C# C# E C# B B A A B G# B A
O na . yum Se mma ri yum On . dra . ga Me . yya Sei vom . . . .
DF#,A, BD,F#, C#E,A, DF#,A,

70
G A D
G# A A A G# A D B A G E F# A E F# E D
Then . na na E . nnan . ga le . U lla . thil Paay chi du vom
DF#,A, BD,G, C#E,A, DF#,A,

74
A D G
A A A A C# B C# D F# A F# A A A A B A B A G
U lla . thil Paay . chi du vom Ha lle . lu ja Ha lle Ha lle . . lu ja
C#E,A, DF#,A, D E F# G A B D E F# G

4 Puttham Pudhu

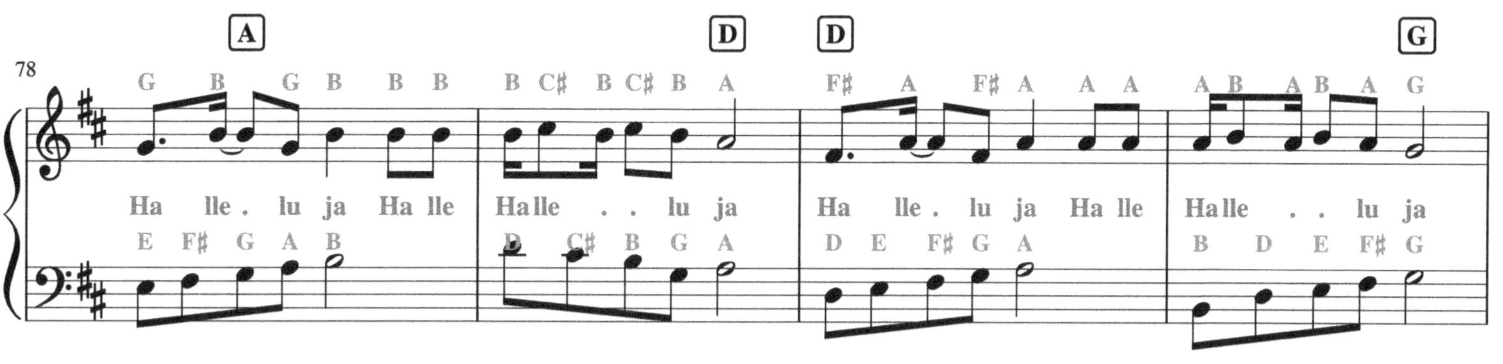

A
D
D
G
Ha lle . lu ja Ha lle
Halle . . lu ja
Ha lle . lu ja Ha lle
Halle . . lu ja

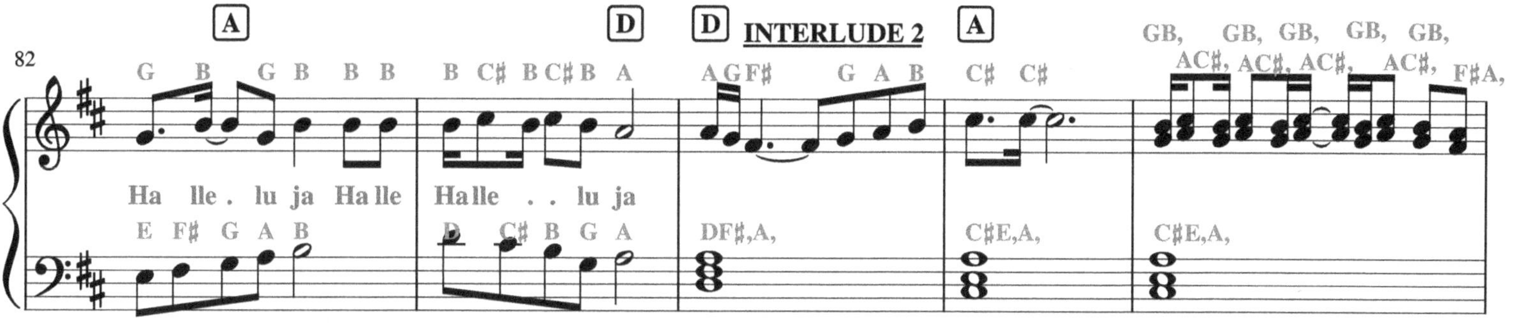

A
D
D INTERLUDE 2
A
Ha lle . lu ja Ha lle
Halle . . lu ja

G
A

D

Ratchagar Pirandare " Am "
christian devotional
www.vp3.in whatsapp +91 8123235873
Music : Jonah BakthaKumar
Transcribed By
Vp3 Music Notes & Karaoke
= 102
INTRO
62

F G Am
Am PALLAVI
12
C B A G B A G F E F G A E F G A E F G A E F G A E F G A E F G A   E E E F F G A
A,F,C B,G,D A,E,C A,E,C
Rat cha gar Pi ran dha re
G C G F C
15
B C B A G C G G G B B F F F F F A G F F E
Beth la ha mi le Vaaazh tha In dru Ma ni dha ra ga Bhoo mi yil Pi ran dha re
B,G,D G,E,C B,G,D A,F,C G,E,C
Am G C G
18
E E E F F G A B C B A G C G G G B B F F F
Rat cha gar Pi ran dha re Beth la ha mi le Vaaazh tha In dru Ma ni dha ra ga
A,E,C B,G,D G,E,C B,G,D
F C Am G Dm F
21
F F A G F F E C D E F E D B C D E D C A B C B
Bhoo mi yil Pi ran dha re Pu dhu Ma lar Poo ka . . Na ru ma na Vee sa . . I dha yan gal
A,F,C G,E,C A,E,C B,G,D A,F,D A,F,C
Am Dm G Em Am
24
A D B C B A B A G A G F E E E E F F G A
Vaazh tha . . I rai ma gan Van dha Christ mas Naa li le Rat cha gar Pi ran dha re
A,E,C A,F,D B,G,D B,G,E A,E,C

Beth la ha mi le
Vaaazh tha In dru Ma ni dha ra ga
Bhoo mi yil Pi ran dha re
INTERLUDE - 1
info.vp3@gmail.com
whatsapp +91 8123235873
www.vp3.in
CHARANAM
Pin da ga tthu Ven da nu kku

Thalai . Sai kka I da mi llai . Ma di da la Pu di lindha ne Pu lla di Ki dai tha dhu
Pin da ga tthu Ven da nu kku
. Thalai . Sai kka I da mi llai . Ma di da la Pu di lindha ne Pu lla di Ki dai tha dhu Na mai
Meet ka . E zhai U ra vil I mma no . Ve lan Van dhan I may Po le . Nammai Kaa ka . . . I rai
Ma ga naay . In gu Pi ran dhan A nnai Ma da lin Thaa laa til Ka nnai Moo di Thoon gi du ven

INTERLUDE - 2
Vi nnil Mi nnum . Thaa ran ga le llam .
Kan gal Si mi tti . . . Si ri thi da ve
Rat cha gar Pi ran dha re
Beth la ha mi le
Vaaazh tha In dru Ma ni dha ra ga
Bhoo mi yil Pi ran dha re

Saavai Vendraar " F "

easter song

www.vp3.in whatsapp +91 8123235873

Eb F F Bb
17
G G Eb Eb Eb F F F F F   C C Bb Bb A Bb Bb Bb Bb Bb
Ha lle lu . ja . Ha lle lu . ja   Ha lle lu . ja . Ha lle lu , ja
EbG,Bb,   CF,A,   CF,A,   DF,Bb,

Eb F BIT RHYTHM F
19
G G Eb Eb Eb F F F F F   F F G G A A
Ha lle lu . ja . Ha lle lu . ja   Saa . vai Ven . drar .
EbG,Bb,   CF,A,   CF,A,

Eb F Eb
23
A A A G G F F Eb   F F G G A A A A A G G F F Eb
Sa ri thi ram Pa dai . thar .   Saa vai . Ven . drar Sa ri thi ram Pa dai tha r.
CF,A,   EbG,Bb,   CF,A,   CF,A,   EbG,Bb,

Cm Eb F
25
Eb Eb Eb Eb F G G G F F F   A A G G F   G A Bb
So nna ba di . . U yir The zhun dhar   Ye su Aan . da var . Nam . .
CEb,G,   EbG,Bb,   EbG,Bb,   CF,A,   CF,A,

27
Bb C G G F   A A G G F   G A Bb Bb C G G F
Ye su Aan , da var .   Ye su Aan . da var . Nam . .   Ye su Aan , da var .
CF,A,   CF,A,   CF,A,

2 Saavai Vendrar

3 Saavai Vendrar

42
F   Bb   Eb   F   Eb
A GAGF GACBb G FEbG GF   A GAGF G A   A GAGF GF Eb
CF,A,   DF,Bb,   EbG,Bb,   CF,A,   CF,A,   CF,A,   CF,A,EbG,Bb,
whatsapp +91 8123288873

46
F   Bb   Eb   F   Dm Cm   Dm   F   Dm   Bb
A GAGF GACBb G FEbG GF   D F EbD C   D EbD F   D F   D C Bb
CF,A,   DF,Bb,   EbG,Bb,   CF,A,   DF,A,   CEb,G,   DF,A,   CF,A,   DF,A,   DF,Bb,

51
Cm   F   F CHARANAM   Bb
C   G   A   F F F   F F   G F Eb Eb D D   Bb
CEb,G,   CF,A,   CF,A,   DF,Bb,
U la gam   U yar kka U yit the zhun dhar   .

53
Cm   F HUMMING BIT Bb   Eb   F
Bb D D Eb F   Eb D C C C   F   G A Bb   G F Eb G F
DF,Bb,   CEb,G,   CF,A,   DF,Bb,   EbG,Bb,   CF,A,
U nna da Vaazh vai   Na ma kka zhai thar

56
Bb
F   F   F   F F   G   F   Eb   D   D   F   D   C   Bb
CF,A,   DF,Bb,
U la gam   U yar kka U yir The zhun dhar . . .

Cm
F
Bb
57
Bb D D Eb F Eb D C C C
F F F G F F Eb D D F D C Bb
U nna dha Vaazh vai Na ma kka zhai thar
Nee dhi Nya yam . Se li thi da ve . . .
DF,Bb,
CEb,G,
CF,A,
DF,Bb,

Cm
F
Eb
59
Bb D D Eb F Eb D C C C
A A G G F G G G F Eb
U yir Pin Vazhi ya A ru la li thar
Ye su Dee . pam En dre . . . . .
DF,Bb,
CEb,G,
CF,A,
EbG,Bb,

F
Eb
61
A A C G G G G A F
A A G G F G G G F Eb
U la gam Mu zhu dhum Sol . vom
Ye su Vazhi . uil thaa ne . . . . .
CF,A,
CF,A,
CF,A,
EbG,Bb,

F
F
Bb
63
Bb C G G G A F
C C Bb Bb A Bb
Mee tu Van . dhom En . bom
Un mai En . drum Vaa zhum
CF,A,
CF,A,
CF,A,
DF,Bb,

Eb
F
F
Bb
65
G G G Eb Eb Eb F
C C Bb Bb A Bb
U la gai Naa . lum Vaa zhum
Un mai En . drum Vaa zhum
EbG,Bb,
CF,A,
CF,A,
DF,Bb,

Eb F F Eb
67
G G G Eb Eb Eb F F F G G A A A A G G F F Eb
U la gai Naa . lum Vaa zhum Saa vai . Ven drar Sa ri thi ram Pa dai tha r.
EbG,Bb, CF,A, CF,A, CF,A, EbG,Bb,
Cm Eb F
69
Eb Eb Eb Eb F G G G F F F A A G G F G A Bb
So nna ba di . . U yir The zhun dhar Ye su Aan . da var . Nam . .
CEb,G, EbG,Bb, EbG,Bb, CF,A, CF,A,
71
Bb C G G F A A G G F G A Bb Bb C G G F
Ye su Aan , da var . Ye su Aan . da var . Nam . . Ye su Aan , da var .
CF,A, CF,A, CF,A,
F Bb Eb F
74
C C Bb Bb A Bb Bb Bb Bb Bb G G Eb Eb Eb F F F F F
Ha lle lu . ja . Ha lle lu , ja Ha lle lu . ja . Ha lle lu . ja
CF,A, DF,Bb, EbG,Bb, CF,A,
F Bb Eb F
76
C C Bb Bb A Bb Bb Bb Bb Bb G G Eb Eb Eb F F F F F
Ha lle lu . ja . Ha lle lu , ja Ha lle lu . ja . Ha lle lu . ja
CF,A, DF,Bb, EbG,Bb, CF,A,
6 Saavai Vendra

Thoongauvadhu Pol " D "
devotional
www.vp3.in whatsapp +91 8123235873
Music : Fr STA Raja
Transcribed By
Vp3 Music Notes & Karaoke
♩ = 150
INTRO

Tho on gu va dhu P o l Tho on gu gi
raa n Kanna i Ennai . Vi lai yaa ttu Vai yam
Tha an gi de Thaa yu m Ne e Al la vo a U na kku
E ni n d a Thaa laa ttu Ura n ga ama l Nee En nai
Yo s i ki rai Ul la thil En ne n na Yaa si ki rai

Ura n ga ama l   Ne e E nna i   Yo si ki rai   U lla thil   En ne n na
Yaa si ki ra a i . .   Dei va thil   Na a dha m e .   Die va
Ba a n a me .   Dei va thil   Na a dh me . . . .   .
Dei va Ba a n a me .   Tho on gu va dhu P o l
Tho on gu gi raa n   K an na i   E nn a i .   Vi lai yaa

INTERLUDE - 1
ttu Vai yam Tha an gi de Thaa yu m Ne e Al la vo a
U na kku E ni n d a Thaa laa ttu
4 Thoonguvadhu

CHARANAM
A dan gaa dha Ka da lil
Pu yal Kaat ru Na du vil
A lai yaa dum Pa da ge ri
O ra than Kol vaan
A dan gaa dha Ka d a lil
Pu yal Kaat ru Na du vil
A lai yaa dum
Pa da ge ri O ra than Kol vaan
I rai Than dhai Ma na dh ai

156
D A7 D
D A A F# / F# E F# E D / C# C# E G / C# C# E A G / F# E F# E D
Ni ram Kaa na / Ven d u m / I ra ve lla / Mu ra ven nu m / Un nai Tha e du
A,F#,D / A,G,E,C# / A,F#,D

161
F# D A7
D / Bb Bb Bb A / Bb Bb Bb D / D A A F# / F# E F# E D / C# C# E G
vaan / I rai Than dhai / Ma na dh ai / Ni ram Kaa na / Ven d u m / I ra ve lla
A#,F#,C# / A,F#,D / A,G,E,C#

167
D
C# C# E A G / F# E F# E D D / F# E E D / F# E E D
Mu ra ven nu m / Un nai Tha e du vaan / I ra kat tum / I dha ya thil
A,F#,D / A,F#,D

172
A Em A D
F# E E D / C# E / G F# F# E / G F# F# E / A G G F# / E F#
Ni rai thi kku / dhaa no / U ra kkat tum / Vi du thi kku / U n Thit tam / Yaa ro
A,F#,D / A,E,C# / B,G,E / A,E,C# / A,F#,D

178
A Em
F# E E D / F# E E D / F# E E D / C# E C# E / G F# F# E
I ra kat tum / I tha ya thil / Ni rai thi kku / dh aa n o / U ra kat tum
A,F#,D / A,F#,D / A,E,C# / B,G,E

183
A D A Bm
G F# F# E A G G F# E F# D D D D C# E D C# B
Vi du thi kku U n Thit tam Yaa ro Dei va thil N aa dha m e .
A,E,C# A,F#,D A,F#,D A,E,C# B,F#,D
Em D D A
E F# G F# E F# D D D D D D C# E D C# B B D C# B
Die va B aa n a me . Dei va thil N aa dh me . . . .
B,G,E A,F#,D A,F#,D A,E,C#
Bm Em D
B E F# G F# E F# D D E F# F# F# F# F# F# A
. Dei va B aa n a me . Tho on gu va dhu P o l
B,F#,D B,G,E A,F#,D D A F# A E
G E E C# C# B B C# C# B B E E Eb F# E D D D
Tho on gu gi raa n K an na i E n n a i . Vi lai yaa
A A G E C# B A A A D A C# D A F# A
D D E E F# F# F# F# F# A G E E C# C# B
ttu Vai yam Tha an gi de Thaa yu m Ne e Al la vo a
E D A F# A E A A G E C# B A

D INTERLUDE - 2 G Em
214
Bm A D G Em Bm A F#
220
Bm Em A F#
228
Bm E A D
235
Em A A Em D
243
U na kku E ni n d a Thaa laa ttu
whatsapp +91 8123235873
info.vp3@gmail.com
www.vp3.in
8 Thoonguvadhu

Uyirthezhundar " A "

devotional

www.vp3.in whatsapp+91 8123235873

E   D   E   C3   Bm   A
21
A A C# D E   F# E D F# E   E F# G#   A B.   C# D C# B G# A
U yir the zhun dar   U yir the zhun dar Ka a   vee ri da n   U yir the zhun dar
A,E,C#   B,G#,E   A,F#,D   B,G#,E   G#,E,C#   B,F#,D   A,E,C#

D   E   Bm   C#
25
C# C# C# C# C#   D D D D D   B A G#   A B.   B C# D C# C# C#
U yir the zhun dar   U yir the zhun dar Na m   Ye su Raja n   U yir the zhun dar
C#,A,E   A,F#,D   B,G#,E   B,F#,D   G#,E,C#

A   D   E   Bm   A
29
C# C# C# C# C#   D D D D D   B A G#   A B.   B B A A A
U yir the zhun dar   U yir the zhun dar Na m   Ye su Raja n   U yir the zhun dar
C#,A,E   A,F#,D   B,G#,E   B,F#,D   C#,A,E

E   D   E   C3   Bm   A
33
A A C# D E   F# E D F# E   E F# G#   A B.   C# D C# B G# A
U yir the zhun dar   U yir the zhun dar Ka a   vee ri Mainda n   U yir the zhun dar
A,E,C#   B,G#,E   A,F#,D   B,G#,E   G#,E,C#   B,F#,D   A,E,C#

INTERLUDE - 1   D   E   A   D   E
37
A C# D C#   D F# A G#   B G# E   D,A,F#   G# E   A C# D C#   D F# A G#
A,E,C#   A,F#,D   B,G#,E   B B B D   C#   A,E,C#   A,F#,D   B,G#,E

INTERLUDE - 1

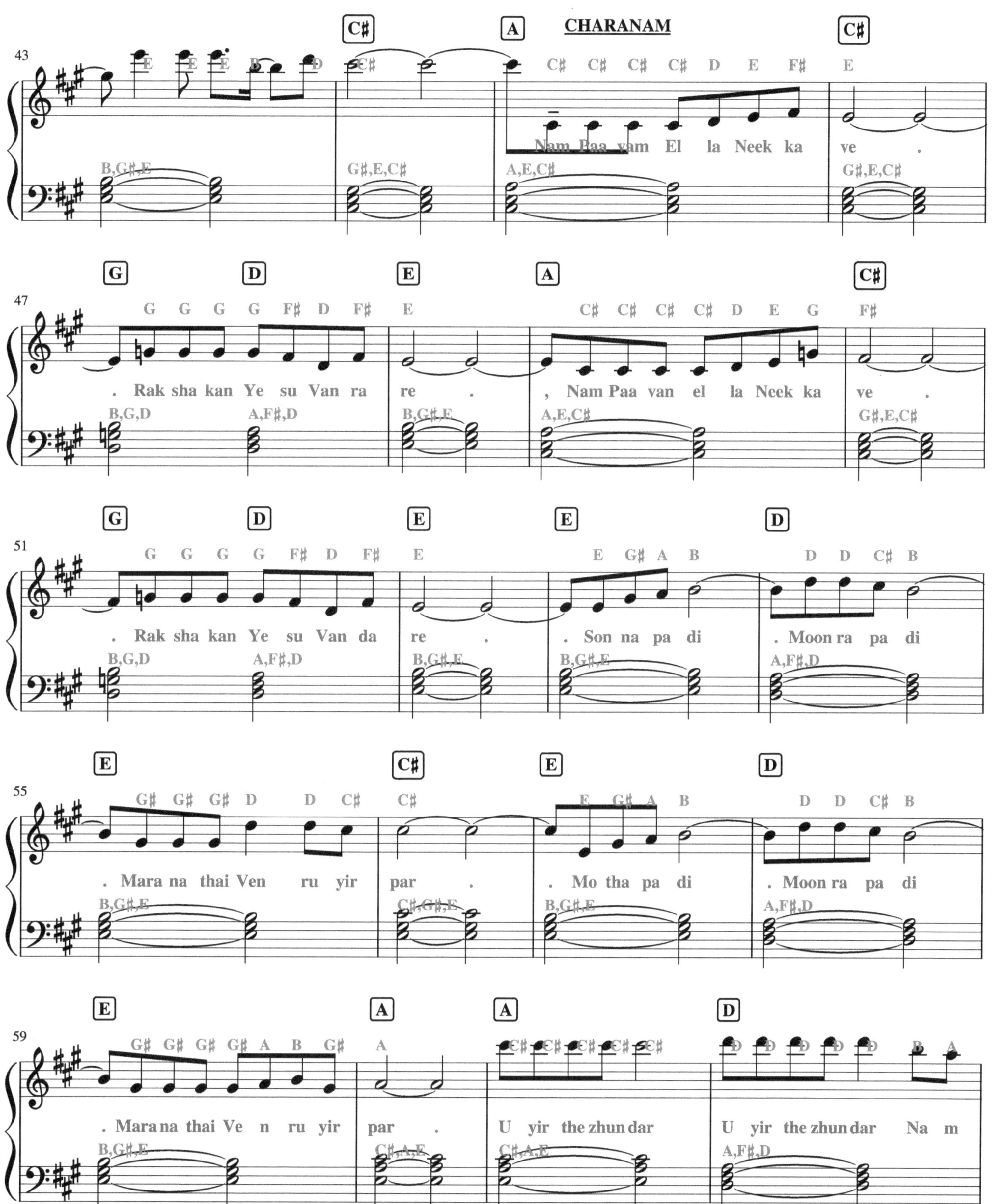

CHARANAM
C#
A
C#
Nam Paa yam El la Neek ka ve .
B,G#,E
G#,E,C#
A,E,C#
G#,E,C#
G
D
E
A
C#
. Rak sha kan Ye su Van ra re . , Nam Paa van el la Neek ka ve .
B,G,D
A,F#,D
B,G#,E
A,E,C#
G#,E,C#
G
D
E
E
D
. Rak sha kan Ye su Van da re . . Son na pa di . Moon ra pa di
B,G,D
A,F#,D
B,G#,E
B,G#,E
A,F#,D
E
C#
E
D
. Mara na thai Ven ru yir par . . Mo tha pa di . Moon ra pa di
B,G#,E
C#,G#,E
B,G#,E
A,F#,D
E
A
A
D
. Mara na thai Ve n ru yir par . U yir the zhun dar U yir the zhun dar Na m
B,G#,E
C#,A,E
C#,A,E
A,F#,D
3 Uyirthezhundhar

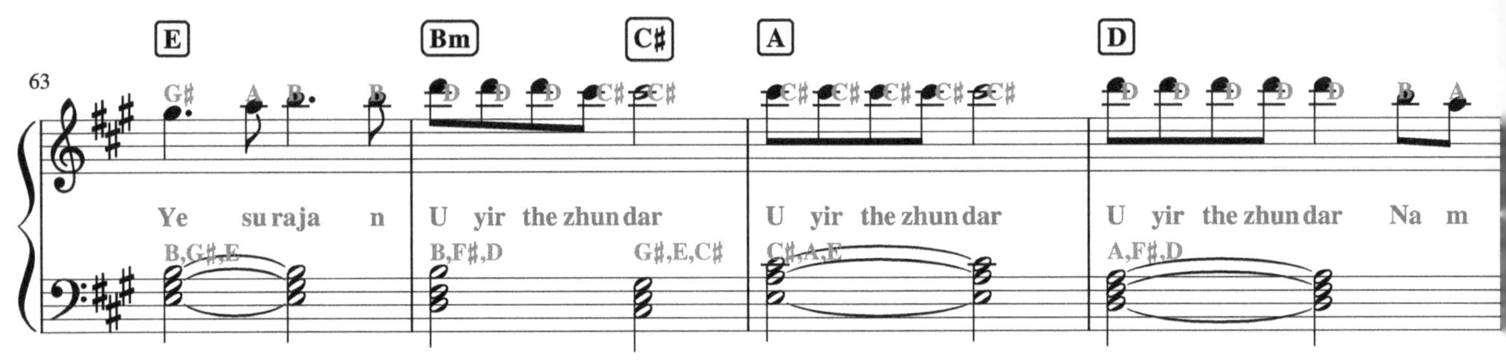

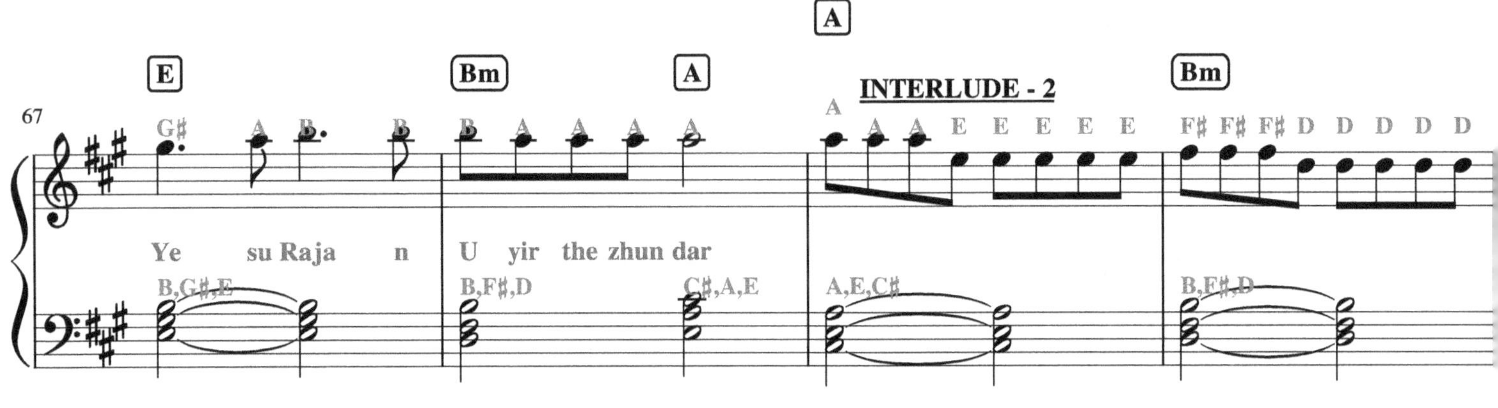

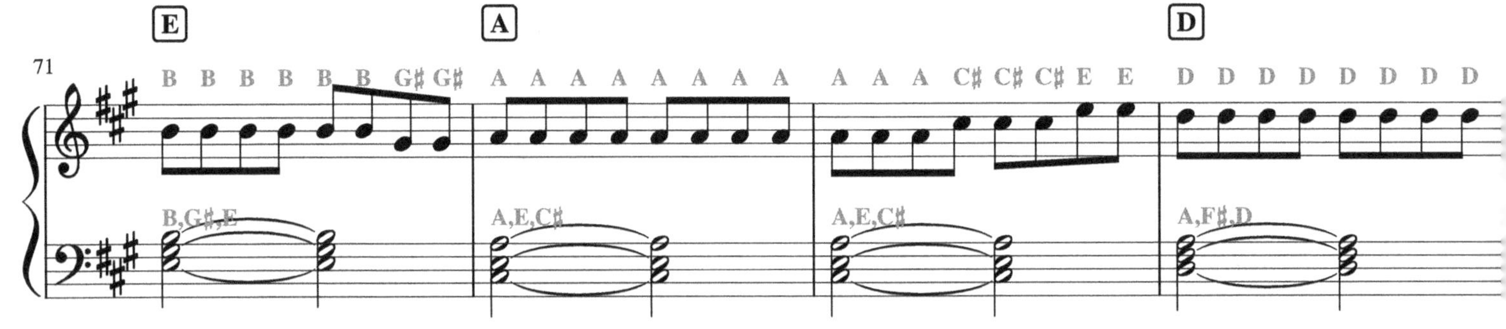

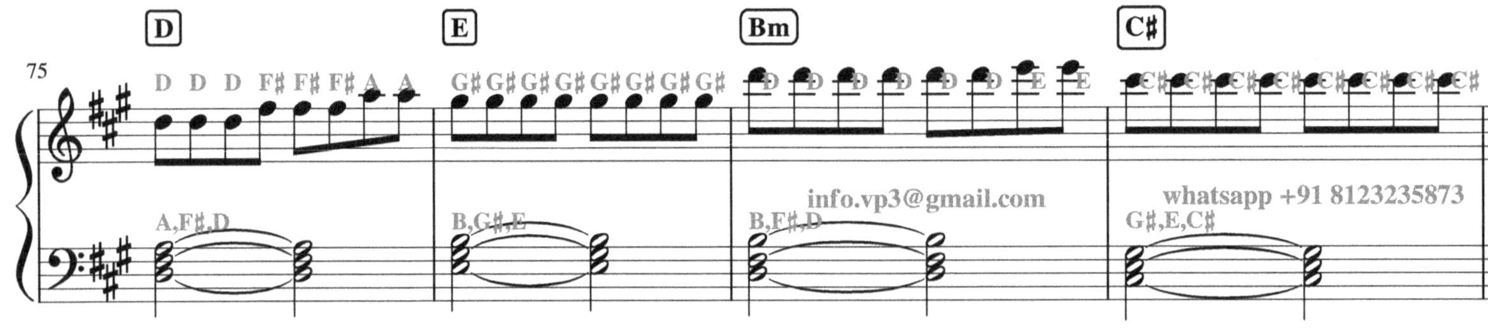

4 Uyirthezhundha

Vaanamum Bhoomiyum " D "

devotional

www.vp3.in whatsapp +91 8123235873

Transcribed By
Vp3 Music Notes & Karaoke

85

Vaa r tha yal U la gai
Kaa ppa va re
Pa ar Po trum Ven dha ne Pa ra ma Ra ja ve
Aa Aa Aa
Paa r Po trum Ven dha ne Pa ra Ra ja ve
Paa vi yai Mee t ka Paa ri nil Van dha va ne

21
A   A G# E   F# F#   A   E F# C# E   E   D
Vaa   . na mum Bhoo mi yum   Pa dai . tha va ne   .
DF#,A,   C#E,A,   DF#,A,

23
A   C# D C# E   E   E   E   C# E   F# G# A G# F# E D
. Vaa . r . thai yal U la gai   Kaa . ppa va re . . . .
C#E,A,   DF#,A,

25
D   D D A   A   A   E F# A F# E C# E D   A C# D F# A C# D F#
. Vaa . na mum Bhoo mi yum   Pa dai . tha va re .   .
DF#,A,   C#E,A,   DF#,A,   DF#,A,

28
D D   D C# B   C# D   C# C# C# B G# B C#
Sa ra . nam . Sa ra nam   Sa ra . nam . Sa ra nam
DF#,A,   EG#,B,C#.

E6

30
F# G#   B C# D   D D   D C# B   C# E D
. Sa ra . na ma yya   . Sa ra . nam . Sa ra . nam
C#F#,A,   DF#,A,   DF#,A,

F#m   D

E6
F#m
D
32
C# C# C# B G# B B E D C#
F# A B C# D
Sa ra . nam . Sa ra . nam . . . . Sa ra . na ma yya
EG#,B,C#, C#F#,A, DF#,A,

INTERLUDE - 1
F#m
D
A
D
34
D A G#A G#A F#G# E C# E F# F# C# B A A G#A E A G# G#A F#
DF#,A, C#F#,A, DF#,A, DF#,A, C#E,A, DF#,A,

F#m7
E
D
A
E
38
C#E F# G# A G#A F# G#B C#D D C#B A C#D C#B G#A F#G#F#
F#A,C#,E, EG#,B, DF#,A, C#E,A, EG#,B,
info.vp3@gmail.com

D
E CHARANAM
41
D F# G#A D C#A F#D C#A F# G# B B B B G#B B B A
Sa ma . dha na Pra bu . ve .
DF#,A, EG#,B,
whatsapp
+91 8123235873

A
43
G#A F#G# A A A E F# A F# D C# C#E F#
. Sa ga . la mum Sey ba va re . Sa ri . tthi ra Naa ya ga ne .
EG#,B, C#E,A,

4 Vanamum Bhumiyum

45
E
D
E
G♯ B   C♯ B   A G♯ F♯ C♯ B   A
G♯ B   B B   G♯ B   B B   B A
. Peri . ya var Nee . . . . re
. Sa maa . dha na Pra . bhu . ve .
EG♯,B,
DF♯,A,
EG♯,B,

47
A
G♯ A   D B   A F♯   A A   A
E F♯   A F♯   D C♯   C♯ E   F♯
. SA ga . la mum Sey . ba va re
. Sa ri . tthi ra Naa . ya ga ne
EG♯,B,
C♯,E,A,

49
E
D
G♯ B   C♯ B   D   D
D D   D C♯   B   C♯   D
. Peri . ya var Nee . re
SA ra . nam . SA ra nam
EG♯,B,
DF♯,A,
DF♯,A,

51
E6
F♯m
D
C♯ C♯   C♯ B   G♯ B   C♯
F♯ G♯   B C♯   D
. SA ra nam . . SA ra nam
. Sa ra . na m yya
EG♯,B,C♯,
C♯F♯,A,
DF♯,A,

53
E6
D D   D C♯   B   C♯ E   D
C♯ C♯   C♯ B   G♯ B   C♯ B E   D C♯
. Sa ra . nam . Sa ra nam .
. SA ra . nam . Sa ra . nam . . .
DF♯,A,
EG♯,B,C♯,

5 Vanamum Bhumiyum

PLAY FULL PALLAVI
INTERLUDE - 2
6 Vanamum Bhumiyun
Sa ra . na ma yya
90

CHARANAM 1 & 2
(Play Charanam 3 till Saranamayya)
INTERLUDE 3
whatsapp +91 8123235873

Vaanil Sangeedham " G "

christmas song

www.vp3.in whatsapp +91 8123235873

Transcribed By
Vp3 Music Notes & Karaoke

Bm
Em
Am
G
16
D C B A B B B
A B B A G G
. Ma nni . thil SAn dho sham
. Swar . gam Thu ra nnu
Cm6
Em
G
D#
A
C
18
F# G F# A G F# E G G G
G F# F# A
Su vi she sha vu . may Glo ri ya
. . . In Excel sis De
D#
Em
G
F#
E
C
21
G G A B
C B A B
vuz . Glo ri ya . . . Glo . ri .
Em
G
G
Bm
24
G
G A
B B B
D C B A
ya . . . Vaa nil San gee tham . Ma nni . thil
Em
Am
G
Cm6
27
B B B A B B
A G G F# G F# A G F#
SAn dho sham . Swar . gam Thu ra nnu Su vi she sha vu .
2 Vaanil Sangeetham

Em   G   D#   A   C   D#
29
E G G G
G F# F# A G
may Glo ri ya . . . In Excel sis De vuz
E G B G B D B   D# G Bb G   A C# E C#   C E G E   D# G Bb G

Em   G   F#   E   C   Em
32
G A B
C B A B G
. Glo ri ya . . . Glo ri ya
E G B G   G B D B   F# Bb C# Bb   E G# B G#   C E G E   E G B G

G   Bm   Cm6   Em
35
INTERLUDE - 1
G A B
whatsapp +91 8123235873
E
G B D B   G B D B   G B D B   G B D B   G B D B   B D F# D   C E G B   E G B G

C#dim7   F   D
39
B A G E F# G A B G   E   B A G E F# G A B G   E   F   F# D   D
E G B G   E G B G   E G B G   C# E G E   C# E G F A C D   F# A F#

G
42
C# D   C# D   C# D   C# D   C# D   E D C B   E D C
D   D F#   A F# D   F#   A F#   D   F#   A F# G   B D B

44
Am
B
C
D
G
Bm
D
G
Am
D
Cm6
Em
G
CHARANAM
Sar va cha ra
F#7
C
G
cha ra vum . . Sa ka la Ja na va li yum . Mok sham
4 Vaanil Sangeetham

Pul . ku vam . Naa . dhan . Vaa ni tha . Ban . dhi tha
ram . Ja nam . . Pee . di tha raa ya var . Pa . pi ka
le . va . rum . Saan . thi Nu kar nni dum . Na . vya San
SAn dhe sha mi tha Thannoo . . . Rak . sha ka nay
. . . Vaa nil Sangee tham . Ma nni . thil SAndho sham . Swar . gam
www.vp3.in
info.vp3@gmail.com
5 Vaanil Sangeetham
96

INTERLUDE - 2
Thura nnu Su vi she sha vu . may Glo ri ya . . . In
Excel sis De vuz . Glo ri ya .
. Glo . ri . ya
6 Vaanil Sangeetham

7 Vaanil Sangeetham
98

Vaigarai Vaaname " Dm "
christian songs
www.vp3.in whatsapp +91 8123235873
Transcribed By
Vp3 Music Notes & Karaoke
= 140
INTRO
PALLAVI
Vai kka ra i Vaa na ma l M e gha Po o kka lla l
Vi di yum Ko la m P o du Ma ra na Irul ve nr u
Veli ch cha ve l la ma ay Ye su va i tho ru In ru
99

F
C
Bb
A A A A A C C C C C C D D D D A A A F
Et tra tha zh vu ga l I ni yum Il lai ya l Vi du tha lai Gee than gal
A,F,C
G,E,C
Bb,F,D
Dm
G INTERLUDE - 1
E F E F E D D D B B A B B A G A A G G E D E
Bu vi en gum Mu zhun gum
A,F,D
B,G,D
B B B B B B B B B D B B A A B B A G A A G G E D E
B,G,D
B,G,D
www.vp3.in
Dm
C
B B B B B B B B B G,E,C A,F,D A D G E
B,G,D
C
D
A,F,D
G,E,C
Dm
C
Dm
F E F E F E F C C D A D G E F E F E F E F
A,F,D
A,F,D
A,F,D
G,E,C
A,F,D

Dm
CHARANAM
40
D E F G A B C D E F G A B C D
D   A   A G   A G   A
Vaan Ma zhai In gu van thu
A,F,D
whatsapp +91 8123235873
A,F,D
42
C
F
Am
D   A   A G A G A   G A G F F G E F   A
Vaazhum mu rai So li than thu Ma nnu kke nna Than nai than dha dae
A,F,D
G,E,C
A,F,C
A,E,C
Dm
45
D   A   A G A G A   D   A   A G A G A
Thaan En num En nam Nee ki Naam En num Kol gai Kon daal
A,F,D
A,F,D
47
C
F
Am
Dm
G A G F F G E F   A   D   D F   F E D
Man nil Naa lum Maat ram Thon ru mae.   Neethi Ni la i thi du m
G,E,C
A,F,C
A,E,C
A,F,D
50
D D F F G A   D   D F   F E D   D D F F G A
Boo mi Nimirn di du m   Vaa nam va sam pa du m Vaa zhvu va la pa dum
A,F,D
A,F,D
A,F,D
3 Vaigarai Vaaname

53
C   G7   Dm   C   G   Dm   C   G
A A C B B B A   A A D C B B B A   A A C B B B A
Be than gal Il laa d a   Ve dan ga l Vaa zh vaa ga   So gan gal Soo zh kin ra
A,F,D G,E,G B,G,F,D   A,F,D G,E,C B,G,D   A,F,D G,E,C B,G,D
56
Dm   C   G   Am   Gm   F   Dm
A A D C B B B A   A G F G G F E   F F E C D
Me gan ga l I ni maa ra   Boomi k ku Ve dam son na   Thiru naal Idu thaa ne
A,F,D G,E,C B,G,D   A,E,C Bb,G,D   A,F,C A,F,D
Dm   INTERLUDE - 2   Am   C
59
A,F,D A D A,F,D   A D D C D F G A   G F G F
D D D   D D D   A,F,D A,E,C G,E,C
Dm   Am   C   Dm
63
D F C D F G A   G F G F A   A Bb A G F E D   A A Bb A G F E D
A,F,D A,E,C G,E,C   A,F,D   A,F,D
67
D A Bb C D E F G E F G A Bb C D
A,F,D   info.vp3@gmail.com
4 Vaigarai Vaaname

1. ILAYARAJA HITS	29. V. HARIKRISHNA HITS
2. AR RAHMAN HITS	30. TAMIL OLD HITS
3. LATEST TAMIL HITS	31. ARJUN JANYA HITS
4. HARRIS JAYARAJ HITS	32. KANNADA OLD HITS
5. GV PRAKASH KUMAR HITS	33. KANNADA RAJKUMAR HITS
6. SP BALASUBRAMAYAM HITS	34. D IMAN TAMIL ITS
7. SANTHOSH NARAYANAN HITS	35. SID SRIRAM HITS
8. THAMAN S HITS	36. ILAYARAJA TAMIL HITS
9. DEVISRI PRASAD HITS	37. CHIRANJEEVI HITS
10. KANNADA HITS	38. SPB KANNADA HITS
11. HOLYWOOD HITS	39. S. JANAKI HITS
12. S. JANAKI TAMIL HITS	40. ILAYARAJA MALAYALAM HITS
13. MALAYALAM HITS	41. SHREYA GHOSHAL KANNADA HITS
14. GOPI SUNDAR HITS	42. YESUDAS HITS
15. ANIRUDH RAVICHANDER HITS	43. KOKILA MOHAN HITS
16 HARIHARAN HITS	44. OP NAYYAR HITS
17. HARRIS JAYARAJ HITS	45. TM SOUNDARAJAN HITS
18. VIDYA SAGAR HITS	46. MSV HITS
19. RAVEENDRAN HITS	47. GOLDEN GANESH HITS
20. UDIT NARAYANANA HITS	48. NTR & BALAKRISHNA HITS
21 SONU NIGAM HITS	49. ARMAN MALIK HITS
22 THEME MUSIC	50. TELUGU OLD HITS
23 YUVAN HITS	51. MALAYALAM OLD HITS
24 CHRISTIAN SONGS	52. MALAYALAM CHRISTIAN SONGS
25 CHITRA HITS	53. ALLU ARJUN HITS
26. HAMSALEKHA HITS	54. PRITHVI RAJ HITS
27 RAJANIKANTH HITS	55. SHREYA GOSHAL HITS
28 KAMAL HASAN HITS	56. KARTHIK HITS

1. LATEST BOLLYWOOD HITS	29. JEET GANGULY HITS
2. ARJITH SINGH HITS	30. KALYANJI - ANANDJI HITS
3. ARMAN MALIK HITS	31. NADHEEM – SHRAVAN HITS
4. SHREYA GHOSHAL HITS	32. NAUSHAD ALI HITS
5. KUMAR SANU HITS	33. AMITAB BACCHAN HITS
6. UDIT NARAYANAN HITS	34. DILEEP KUMAR HITS
7. SONU NIGAM HITS	35. NUSRAT FATEH ALI KHAN HITS
8. MOHD RAFI HITS	36. OP NAYYAR HITS
9. LATA MANGESHKAR HITS	37. PANKAJ MULLICK HITS
10. MUKESH KUMAR HITS	38. KRISHNARAO PHULAMBRIKAR HITS
11. HOLYWOOD HITS	39. DALER MEHENDI HITS
12. JAGAJITH SINGH HITS	40. RAAM LAKSHMAN HITS
13. PANKAJ UDHAS HITS	41. RANJIT BAROT HITS
14. MADAN MOHAN HITS	42. RAKESH ROSHAN HITS
15. ANKIT TIWARI HITS	43. ROOP KUMAR RATHOD HITS
16. PREETHAM HITS	44. SANJIB SARKAR HITS
17. AJAY ATUL HITS	45. SALIL CHOUDARY
18. ASHA BONSLE HITS	46. SAJID – WAJID HITS
19. RD BURMAN HITS	47. SANDEEP CHOWTA HITS
20 SD BURMAN HITS	48. SHANKAR - EHSANN – LOY HITS
21. RAJESH KHANNA HITS	49. SHANKAR – JAIKISHAN HITS
22. ADNAN SAMI HITS	50. SOHAIL SEN HITS
23. ANURADHA PAUDWAL HITS	51. UTTAM SINGH HITS
24. AMIT TRIVEDI HITS	52. VIJU SHAH HITS
25. LAKSHMIKANTH - PYARELAL HITS	53. VISHAL BARADHWAJ HITS
26. RAJKAPOOR HITS	54. ADITYA SRIVASTAV HITS
27. DATTA DAVJEKAR HITS	55. VISHAL – SHEKAR HITS
28. HIMESH RESHAMMIYA HITS	56. AR RAHMAN HITS